Se... ...sion,
he pulle... ...into his arms . . .

His hand, caressing her back, molded her to
him. When she tipped her head back to look at
him expectantly, her lips, moistened to receive
the kiss she was sure would come. He shook
his head. Instead, he brought his hand up
to trace her lips gently, tantalizingly, then
cupped her head and brought it back against
his chest, where the rough wool of his jacket
scratched her sensitive skin.

A tumult of sensations assaulted Melody. Her
knees felt weak and yet, somehow, she knew
she was safe, as long as this enigmatic man
continued to hold her. She'd never felt so
incredibly protected and beloved in her life—
and yet she hardly even knew him!

Bantam Circle of Love Romances
Ask your bookseller for the books you have missed

Dear Friend,

Enter the Circle of Love—and travel to faraway places with romantic heroes . . .

We read hundreds of novels and, each month, select the very best—from the finest writers around the world—to bring you these wonderful love stories . . . stories that let *you* share in a variety of beautiful romantic experiences.

With Circle of Love Romances, you treat yourself to a romantic holiday—anytime, anywhere. And because we want to please you, won't you write and let us know your comments and suggestions?

Meanwhile, welcome to the Circle of Love— we don't think you'll ever want to leave!

Best,

Cathy Camhy
Editor

CIRCLE OF LOVE ™

Images of Love

Alexandra Kirk

BANTAM BOOKS
TORONTO · NEW YORK · LONDON · SYDNEY

IMAGES OF LOVE
A Bantam Book/August 1982
Circle of Love, the garland and the ring designs are
trademarks of Bantam Books, Inc.

ISBN 0-553-21546-9

Published simultaneously in the United States and Canada

Bantam Books are published by Bantam Books, Inc. Its
trademark, consisting of the words "Bantam Books" and the
portrayal of a rooster, is Registered in U.S. Patent and
Trademark Office and in other countries. Marca Registrada.
Bantam Books, Inc., 666 Fifth Avenue, New York, New York
10103.

PRINTED IN THE UNITED STATES OF AMERICA

O   0 9 8 7 6 5 4 3 2 1

For Steve and Eve,
with thanks for our German
odyssey

One

One of the first things Melody had noticed about West Berlin, when she arrived two months ago, was the noise. The city had the same jarring, discordant sounds as her native New York. The clamor of trucks, buses, and hurtling taxicabs had made her feel comfortably at home almost at once.

The noise was unceasing. Even in the middle of the night, the familiar street sounds reached her third-floor apartment and seemed to lull her to sleep. She had become so accustomed to the honking horns and squealing tires, in fact, that it took several minutes for the softer, but equally insistent, sound of the ringing phone to awaken her from her deep sleep.

Glancing at the illuminated dial of her digital clock, she saw it was barely four A.M. A call at that hour could mean only illness or disaster. With a slight shiver of trepidation, she picked up the phone.

"Yes. Hello," she said, her voice still raspy with sleep.

A demanding masculine voice snapped, "Let me speak to M. L. Adamson."

Immediately irritated at the unnecessarily curt tone, Melody snapped right back. "Call back in the morning."

"Morning will be too late. I must speak to Adamson immediately. Stop arguing with me and get him on the line."

"Forget it," she retorted and took a perverse delight in hearing his uttered exclamation just as she slammed the receiver back into the cradle. It was barely back in place, when the phone began ringing again.

Pulling a pillow over her head to muffle the sound, Melody tried to ignore the ringing, but it was a futile effort. She'd spent too many anxious moments waiting for very special phone calls to be able to ignore one now. Even though she knew perfectly well it was the insufferably rude stranger once more, she eventually gave in.

Sighing deeply as she answered, she said, "All right. You win."

"Not yet. Adamson is still not on the line. Now why don't you just be a nice girl and get your lover to the phone. I've got some business to discuss with him."

Swallowing her anger, Melody adopted her sweetest tone. "You know, I may be naive, but I've found that very little legitimate business is conducted at four o'clock in the morning. Would you care to explain what you want?"

"Not to you. I don't have time to waste in order to satisfy your curiosity. And, frankly, I'm surprised he puts up with this sort of interference from you. It can't do his business any good. If you'd just get him for me now, you two could get back to whatever it was you were doing before I interrupted."

"Oh, you didn't interrupt anything," she said blithely. "In fact, I'm all alone here. I'm terribly sorry if that throws a damper on all those romantic images you've conjured up for yourself."

"Blast it all, lady. Do you know how much time we've wasted with all this bickering? Why the devil didn't you just tell me Adamson wasn't there? Where is he and how can I reach him?"

"She," Melody corrected, pausing for emphasis, "is here."

"She," the caller repeated, his aggressiveness finally beginning to ebb away.

"Yes. She. I am M. L. Adamson."

The embarrassed silence that followed this announcement went on so long, Melody thought for a minute the man might have hung up.

Finally he spoke. "I apologize, Miss Adamson. No one told me. I just assumed . . ."

"I know. You assumed I was a man. That's exactly what I want people to think. Amazingly enough, there are a lot of people still who don't wish to hire female photographers. But once they've seen my work, they don't seem to mind so much that my name is Melody, instead of Marvin or Malcolm."

"Well, I'm sorry to have troubled you, Miss Adamson, but I do mind. Good-bye."

"Hey, wait just a minute. I thought you were looking for a good photographer," Melody said quickly.

"I am, but as I said . . ."

"You don't want a woman for the job."

"Exactly. I find it usually complicates things."

"What things?" Melody countered with some asperity. "I am a professional photographer. When I am on an assignment, the only things on my mind are the subject, the lighting, and the camera. If you can't be equally professional, that shouldn't be my problem."

"Ah, but in this case, I think it is. I do not intend to work with some temperamental woman who'll fly into jealous rages without the least provocation or who'll jabber incessantly and spoil my concentration."

"My, my. You must have met some real charmers in your time," Melody said sarcastically. To herself she was beginning to wonder why she was battling so hard for the chance to work with this intractable egomaniac.

Now, in answer to her last observation, he said with a hard edge of bitterness, "You could say that. My experiences with women have left me somewhat jaded. Sorry, Miss Adamson, but that's just the way it is."

"Well, I'm sorry too, but since you've rousted me out of bed in the middle of the night, you might answer just one more question for me."

"All right. One more."

"Have you seen my work?"

"Yes."

"And you liked it?" Melody was unaccountably curious about his impression of her photographs.

"That's two questions, but, yes, I liked it. It was very impressive."

"Tell me, then. What is more important to you, finding the best photographer available for your project or avoiding the risks you feel are involved in working with a woman?"

Melody held her breath, hoping that she'd guessed correctly about the caller's obsession with quality. If his professional ego was as large as his private one, he'd want only the best. In her three years as a free-lance photographer, she'd found that appealing to professional pride often landed the most reluctant accounts.

"You certainly cut right through to the issues, don't you, Miss Adamson," he said with a certain grudging respect. "And you're right. I do want someone who can do more with a camera than merely click the shutter."

Finally, after a lengthy pause, he continued. "All right. The job is yours. But at the first emotional outburst, you are finished. Understood?"

"Absolutely. Thank you, Mister. . . ?"

"Wainwright. Bradley Wainwright."

Melody recognized the name instantly. Bradley Wainwright was a highly respected magazine writer. He roamed the globe for a variety of publications, exploring the richness of an area's history, spotlighting its architectural treasures, and capturing the life-style of its residents. Tiny, previously unpublicized and unnoticed villages came alive with his deft prose.

The pictures that accompanied the articles were always first-rate. Melody had often envied the photographers granted those choice assignments and, now that she had one, she knew she was going to be taxed to the limits of her skills.

Beyond his reputation as a writer, she knew very little about Wainwright. He seemed to shun personal publicity, and only once could she recall having seen his name in some international gossip column, linked to that of an American television news correspondent.

The voice that interrupted her chaotic thoughts was once again impatient. "Miss Adamson, I'll expect you to be ready by eight o'clock. We have a nine-thirty flight to Munich. I'll have a car waiting for us there. Plan on being gone at least two weeks, possibly three. If you've got a boyfriend, put him on hold. There will be no time for anything other than work on this trip."

When he'd finished his list of orders, Melody inquired rather timidly, "Mr. Wainwright, could I ask just one more question?"

"If you're sure it will be just one."

"What's the assignment?" she asked, and was relieved when he actually burst out laughing. It was the hearty sound of a man with a well-practiced sense of humor, something that seemed at odds with Melody's initial impression of Bradley Wainwright as a perpetually irascible old goat. It made him seem younger and possibly even vulnerable.

"That did get lost in the shuffle, didn't it?" he said with some amusement. "It's an article on some of the smaller towns in southern Germany, the ones the tourists always miss in their rush to get to Munich or Frankfurt or the spas of Baden-Baden. It's a beautiful area. I think you'll enjoy it."

"I thought you said there'd be no time for anything other than work," she teased, encouraged by the earlier lightening of his tone. But to her dismay he reverted to his earlier no-nonsense tenor.

"There won't be time for anything other than work, Miss Adamson. I was referring to my impression that most photographers enjoy and admire true beauty as a natural outgrowth of their work."

"Sorry, Mr. Wainwright. Of course we do."

"Fine, then. I'll see you at eight," he said, hanging up so quickly she had no chance to respond.

By now it was nearly five A.M., and Melody knew there was little chance of falling back to sleep. She decided the time would be best spent checking out her equipment and packing.

The latter was actually the easiest part. She'd learned early to carry as few clothes and cosmetics as possible. She could manage only one light suitcase in addition to her camera cases, unless she wanted to rely on porters, and all too frequently there were none to be had in the smaller cities to which she'd traveled.

She threw in her usual assortment of blue jeans

and shirts, then as a last-minute whim added a clinging jersey dress in her favorite shade of turquoise. It was what she wore whenever her self-confidence needed a boost, and she had a feeling the dress was going to be invaluable over the next couple of weeks.

Two

Though she was worn out by her abbreviated night's sleep and some frantic last-minute packing, Melody's spirits were high, buoyed by the prospect of working with Bradley Wainwright. She had worked hard for a break like this, and, if her luck held, it could mean the beginning of many challenging assignments for major magazines.

Until now her free-lance work had been fun, but hardly either stimulating or profitable. A few of her on-the-spot news photographs of political demonstrations had been picked up by the wire services, thanks to some reporters she'd met. These same contacts had helped her line up several newspapers to use her photographs of the fall fashion showings in Paris.

But her best work by far had been a photographic study of an internationally renowned film director, shot on the spectacularly scenic location of his last movie. Unfortunately, this study had done little to add to her list of clients. The photographs, in a small French magazine for the arts, had had only a limited audience.

Melody wondered briefly which of all of her photographs Wainwright had seen. "Oh, well, it hardly matters, as long as I've got the job," she thought.

There was another reason for Melody's high hopes. This assignment could well be the vindication she needed for not having heeded the advice of her aunt back in New York.

"Now perhaps I can convince Aunt Leah that coming to Europe wasn't a mistake."

Melody frowned at the memory of the bitter battle they'd had when she announced her decision to take her small inheritance and spend some time in London, Paris, Vienna, Rome, and now Berlin, trying to make it in the highly competitive world of free-lance photography. Her aunt—a dynamic, well-established newspaper columnist—thought Melody was being foolish in taking such a risk. She'd urged her to reconsider, to begin her career back home, working either for a newspaper or even an advertising agency.

"Then, when you've got some solid experience and some contacts, go out and try to make it on your own," Aunt Leah had begged.

But Melody had been afraid to wait. She was sure that, like so many of her aunt's friends, she would get caught up in a secure routine and never dare to break loose.

"I want to do it now, while I've got nothing to

lose," she'd said, trying to make her aunt understand.

They had always been so close. Even before the accident that had left Melody an orphan at fourteen, Aunt Leah had been her friend and confidante. Afterward, when she'd turned her own life upside down to take care of her grief-stricken niece, Aunt Leah had become even more precious to Melody.

It had been all Melody could do to turn her back on her aunt's well-meaning objections, but she had done it. And now, it seemed, it was finally paying off.

Suddenly Melody realized it was almost eight o'clock. Determined to make a good impression, she gathered up her luggage and equipment and went down to wait in front of the building for Wainwright.

She had been waiting at the curb for more than forty-five minutes and was beginning to fear he'd meant for her to take a taxi to the airport, when a battered old Mercedes finally pulled up.

"Miss Adamson, I presume?" the driver queried in the by-now familiar impatient tone.

At her nod, the passenger door was unceremoniously flung open, and he ordered curtly, "Get in. We're late."

"You're late," she countered. "I've been right here for the last forty-five minutes."

"Miss Adamson, I do not have time to sit here arguing the relative merits of our cases. The fact is that we are both about to miss the flight to Munich. Now, are you getting in or am I going alone?"

To her absolute amazement, he actually began to pull away from the curb.

"Wait. Of course I'm going."

Quickly she tossed her things into the backseat, then climbed in beside him. She barely had the door closed, when he shot off down the street, narrowly missing a woman carrying a basket of eggs and several long, crusty loaves of bread.

Judging her companion's mood to be almost as lousy as his manners and his driving, Melody decided to remain as unobtrusive as possible. The ride, she decided, would provide an excellent opportunity for her to study the man beside her.

Looking at him covertly, she had to admit he was very attractive in a rugged, fierce sort of way. The firm set of his mouth was just what she'd expect from a man who used his bullying tactics. On the other hand, tiny white lines were etched into the tan around his eyes, hinting that he could laugh a good deal. There again was that hint of an intriguing contradiction.

"Like what you see?" he asked finally, his eyes never wavering from the crowded road.

Melody flushed in embarrassment. "I'm sorry. I guess I was being rude."

"Don't apologize. I'm used to it," he said.

"I'll just bet you are," Melody whispered under her breath. Apparently the comment wasn't made quite softly enough.

"I meant, Miss Adamson, that in my line of work I am always arousing an unusual amount of attention. Most of the towns about which I write don't get a lot of tourists, particularly Americans. They are fascinated by foreign writers. And, I'm sure you'll discover, by attractive photographers," he added, giving her a sideways glance.

Their eyes locked, and, to Melody, the air seemed charged with electricity. Finally, a glint of amusement in his eyes, he turned back to the road.

During the silence that followed, Melody grew increasingly uncomfortable. She tried to attribute her nervousness to her companion's disconcertingly bad manners, but that did not explain the stomach-tightening awareness his gaze had aroused in her.

Finally, in an effort to make conversation, she asked, "Just where will we be going? You said something about small towns."

"So I did. Well, we'll have to talk about it later. Right now we're going to have to run like hell to make our plane. Can you carry all that stuff?" he asked skeptically, as he eyed her slight figure.

"Of course. I'm used to it," she said, gathering up the camera cases and her suitcase and striding off toward the terminal, not waiting to see if he followed.

Suddenly he was beside her. "Don't be so blasted independent," he said, trying to smother a grin.

"Just wanted to prove I could do it. You insisted I be able to pull my own weight, you know."

"Your own weight, not your weight in baggage. Come on, let's make a dash for it."

As they passed by the ticket counter without stopping, Melody called out breathlessly, "What about checking in?"

"No time. They'll take care of it at the gate."

They made it with only minutes to spare, as an airline agent quickly scanned their tickets and passports, checked their luggage, and hurried them on board.

The plane was off the ground and the stewardess was taking breakfast orders before Melody's heart returned to its normal pace and her panting ceased.

"Feel better now?" asked the tormentor at her side. "I think perhaps you could use something to drink."

"That would be nice," she admitted, suddenly feeling incredibly weary. "I guess I am a bit out of shape."

"I'd never have guessed it," Wainwright said, his eyes roving over her petite but very obviously feminine figure. His gaze stopped at her breasts, which were rising and falling rhythmically beneath a bright green sweater, which went well with her fair complexion and light brown hair.

Melody was saved from responding by the appearance of the stewardess.

"We'll both have some coffee. Black," her companion said. Then, noticing her look, he added, "Unless, of course, you'd prefer something else."

Melody was tempted to change the order out of sheer obstinacy, but since coffee was exactly what she did want, she finally just shook her head in resignation. "No. That's fine."

When the stewardess had moved on, after giving Bradley Wainwright a beaming smile, Melody turned to him.

"Mr. Wainwright," she began determinedly.

"Oh, oh," he said mockingly. "I've done something wrong?"

"A lot, as a matter of fact. Just because you feel you're doing me some incredible favor by allowing me to work with you does not give you the right to try to take over my life."

"Is that what I was doing? Simply by ordering your drink for you? Come now, Miss Adamson, that was merely a breach of courtesy, nothing more. Hardly the sort of sin you imply."

"Perhaps so, but it is indicative of the sort of overbearing attitude you've had toward me ever since you made that phone call last night. You immediately assumed I was nothing more than some unimportant mistress, who stood between you and the man you thought you were calling."

"I thought I'd apologized for that."

"You did, but your manner still hasn't changed. You're still treating me as though I were somewhat addlepated, just because I'm a woman. I assure you I am reasonably bright and capable. And, since you've seen my photographs, I assume you're at least willing to admit I am more than moderately capable at my profession."

"Unquestionably."

"Then perhaps if we stick strictly to business, we can manage to get along," she suggested. "Look, Mr. Wainwright, I really want this assignment to work out. It could be the most important thing in my career. But I won't be able to do my best, if you're going to be filled with unconcealed doubts every time I aim my camera."

"You've made your point, Miss Adamson," he

conceded grudgingly. "I will try to keep whatever misgivings I may have about this to myself. And I promise to let you place all your own drink orders from now on. Will that do?"

Melody smiled in spite of herself. "It's a beginning," she said, holding out her hand. Her nerves tingled as his much larger hand enveloped hers and held it tightly. The long, lingering look he gave her, before releasing her hand, was unreadable, but once more it seemed to stir an exciting feeling of anticipation in Melody.

She longed to prolong the moment, but Wainwright immediately picked up his briefcase, sorted through some papers, and started working on his notes.

Finally Melody was able to relax enough to doze, but when she did, her dreams were filled with images of the complex man beside her.

Three

Over the next few hours Melody discovered she was not the exclusive target for Bradley Wainwright's sharp tongue and domineering attitude. He blew up upon discovering that their rental car was not ready, then set out to charm the flustered agent into giving them one that was reserved for one of the company's regular clients.

A few minutes later, waiting while he made some long-distance phone calls, she heard him berating a hapless hotel clerk for a foul-up in their reservation for that night. Noting her expression of distaste, he managed a sheepish grin.

"I know. I know. It's probably not the poor fellow's fault," he told her, while he waited for the man to get back on the line. "But this is one of those rare occasions when the honey-and-vinegar adage does not apply. Vinegar, poured on rather heavily, gets better results."

Pausing a minute to listen, he nodded in satisfaction, mumbled his thanks, and then turned back to Melody, as he replaced the receiver.

"See what I mean? We've got a reservation."

"The end justifies the means, I suppose?"

"In this case, yes. Unless you'd prefer to spend the night in a field, sleeping under the stars. Ettal is not exactly midtown Manhattan, with a hotel on every corner. This inn is about all there is."

Seeing that she remained unconvinced, he shrugged. "You'll see. Now, let me make one more call and we'll be on our way."

Although Melody moved out of hearing range, she could not help noticing that there was a decided shift in his mood during this last call. He was talking animatedly, and the conversation was punctuated with that rich, booming laugh. Curious despite herself, Melody drifted closer.

"Yeah, I'll miss you too," she heard him say tenderly. "It won't be that long until Saturday, and I'll see you then. Promise me you'll take good care of yourself, okay?"

Melody felt an unreasonable surge of jealousy toward the unknown recipient of that call. Clearly it was someone with whom he was on very intimate terms. It was also obvious that the woman would be joining them in a few days, a situation that seemed thoroughly unfair to Melody, since she had been warned against planning any time with her boyfriends. Not that she had any. But, still, it was just one more example of Bradley Wainwright trying to dictate one set of rules for her and another for himself.

"Hey! I asked if you were ready to leave," he said, interrupting her thoughts.

"Sure," she said with considerably more docility than she would have liked. "Where are we going first?"

"I thought we'd stop at the market here and pick up some things for lunch. Then we can stop on the way for a picnic."

"On the way to where?" she persisted.

"I do seem determined to keep you in the dark, don't I? Sorry. We're going to Wies first. There's a wonderful pilgrimage church there built by the great architect Dominikus Zimmermann. It's in a meadow that should be filled with wild flowers this time of the year. In the distance you can see the Alps. It's like something right out of *The Sound of Music* . . ."

Melody watched his face as he talked, fascinated with the changes wrought by his obvious enthusiasm. His eyes, which had appeared to her an icy blue, were warmer now, with the sparkle of sapphires. His usual scowl had been erased, replaced by an infectious grin that made him appear more boyish than ever.

Melody had expected a testy, middle-aged sophisticate and, instead, she had found a casual, occasionally kind, man in his thirties. So far, however, she could not revise her original description of testy, she admitted ruefully.

"I'm boring you, aren't I?" he asked, noticing that her mind seemed to be wandering.

"Not at all. I was just trying to recall what I had read about the church. Isn't it his last great masterpiece?"

"Yes. That's the one. He loved it so much that he stayed in a little cottage just a few hundred yards away for the rest of his life."

Just then he spotted a parking place and pulled into it quickly. Turning to her he asked, "Before we waste an entire afternoon wandering through the whole market, do you have any idea what you'd like for lunch?"

"How about bread and cheese? I don't think I've ever had so many wonderful cheeses as I have since coming to Europe."

"Well, let's go see what we can find to tempt you here."

Together they went from stall to stall, selecting huge poppy-seeded rolls, a variety of pungent-smelling cheeses, and an assortment of fresh fruits. The latter were displayed in such geometrically perfect arrangements Melody almost hated to see the symmetry destroyed.

An hour later they were picnicking alongside the Starnberger See, a peaceful lake shrouded in a gray haze but dotted nonetheless by colorful sailboats. A steady procession of ducks waddled up to beg for bits of bread from their lunch.

Laughing, Melody broke off pieces from her roll and fed them. Somehow she was feeling almost giddy with unexplained happiness.

"Tell me something, Melody," Bradley Wainwright said, unexpectedly shattering their companionable silence. "Why are you doing this?"

"Doing what?"

"Struggling to make it as a photographer. Shouldn't you be back home getting married, taking care of kids, going to PTA meetings, instead of galivanting halfway around the world all alone?"

"You're a bit out of touch, aren't you?"

"You mean with the women's movement, equal rights, that sort of thing? No. I'm not out of touch. But you don't seem the type. You don't seem quite tough enough. You strike me as a dabbler, who'll play at taking pictures until the right man comes along. Then you'll chuck it all for marriage, a cozy little cottage, the whole family bit. Am I right?"

"Your head is apparently thicker than I thought," Melody responded angrily. "My photography is every bit as important to me as your writing is to you. Maybe I will get married someday, but that doesn't mean I have to stick my cameras in a closet and take them out only to shoot snapshots at the kids' birthday parties. Women can have homes and careers too, you know.

"What about that correspondent friend of yours, Lesley MacDonald?" she continued, ignoring the look of pain that flashed briefly across his face. "She has a full-time career, doesn't she? People don't land network assignments overseas unless they're dedicated to their jobs. Do you think she'd toss it all over to get married?"

"You don't know what you're talking about," he said stiffly. "Lesley MacDonald is not the issue here. Nor do I care to discuss her with you at any other time. Come on, let's get out of here."

Roughly he gathered up their trash and stuffed it into a nearby container, though Melody felt certain he'd have preferred to stuff it down her throat. Hurt and confused by his sudden anger, she sat huddled in the car as far from him as possible.

"Look," he said finally. "I'm sorry for the outburst. If you'd known me longer, you'd know that Lesley is someone I don't discuss. With anyone. Now let's just drop it."

Although his awkward apology eased the tension somewhat, they rode in silence for the next forty or so kilometers. It was only when they were winding along the narrow road toward Wies that he spoke again.

"We won't have much time here this afternoon. I just want you to get a look at the place, and then we'll come back again. I've already spent a great deal of time here, so I have most of the information I need. But you can wander as much as you like and get a feel for the church and decide what you might want to photograph."

Melody nodded, as he pulled off onto a wide dirt shoulder alongside the road. If one were to judge by the other cars, this apparently served as some sort of parking area, but Melody couldn't see anything nearby. Puzzled, she asked, "We're here?"

"Yes. We have to walk up the road a bit. Are you going to bring your camera?"

"Yes. The lighting's still very good, and I might be able to get started this afternoon."

As they walked over the rise in the road along with a group of tourists who sounded as though they might be Canadian, Melody stopped in her tracks, her eyes wide with wonder.

"It's beautiful," she whispered.

"I told you," he said, clearly pleased by her reaction.

Ahead of them, sitting virtually in the middle of a field of pink and yellow and purple wild flowers, was the church. The snowcapped peaks of the Alps, rising into a deep blue sky, provided the backdrop.

Inside the small church, Melody gasped with pleasure and surprise. It was a tiny, perfectly proportioned example of Rococo architecture, with pastel-painted frescoes and gold-gilt trim everywhere. Although her photographic eye preferred clean, simple lines, the elaborate barrage of colors and design here played to her senses nonetheless.

Bradley Wainwright, instinctively understanding her need to absorb her initial impressions and translate them into a photographic approach that would convey the same sort of awe to magazine readers, left her alone.

Melody wandered, oblivious to the tourists, plotting angles for her pictures and looking for the best natural sources of light. She wanted the feeling of sunlight streaming in from the heavens, rather than the flat look she would get with artificial light.

When she emerged, nearly an hour later, she spotted her companion walking through the field, hands stuffed into the pockets of his tweed jacket, his shoulders hunched forward dejectedly. Uncertain at first whether to approach him, she paused until he spotted her and beckoned for her to join him.

Moving cautiously over the rough ground, she was conscious that his eyes never left her. Reaching him, she looked up at last and returned his gaze, reading in it a look of longing that left her feeling shattered.

Suddenly, as though sensing her confusion, he pulled her into his arms and held her tightly. His hand, caressing her back, molded her to him. When she tipped her head back to look at him expectantly, her lips moistened to receive the kiss she was sure would come, he shook his head. Instead, he brought his hand up to trace her lips gently, tantalizingly, then cupped her head and brought it back against his chest, where the rough wool of his jacket scratched her sensitive skin.

A tumult of sensations assaulted Melody. Her knees felt weak, and yet, somehow, she knew she was safe, as long as this enigmatic man continued to hold her. She'd never felt so incredibly protected and beloved before in her life and yet she hardly even knew this man.

Finally, without speaking, they pulled apart and walked back to the car, their hands clasped. When, just as they were pulling out, a horse-drawn wagon, trimmed with flowers, came along the road bearing a bride and groom, it made the moment seem almost too magical to be true.

Afraid to break the mood, Melody said nothing on the drive to Ettal. She tried, instead, to analyze the feelings that had been aroused in her, but she was afraid to hold them up to too much scrutiny. They seemed so fragile.

When they reached the inn, which nestled in a

little valley of its own with horses grazing nearby, Melody waited in the car while Brad—yes, she could call him that now—registered and then came back for her.

"We're on the fourth floor," he informed her on his return, adding with a sly grin, "and there are only stairs. Think you can make it?"

"What do you think?"

He laughed. "Just checking, my indomitable spirit."

On the fourth-floor landing, he opened the door to a large room at the left and waited for Melody to go in. He followed, putting all of the luggage into a corner, next to a small sofa, upholstered in a faded pink velvet. It look more functional than attractive or comfortable. The bed, with its slightly shabby but colorful down comforter looked considerably more inviting.

When Brad walked over to the window and stepped out onto a postage-stamp-sized balcony, Melody grew puzzled. As he stepped back into the room, she asked, "Where is your room?"

"Here," he said matter-of-factly.

"Then where is my room?"

"Here."

Melody was at first confused; then, as the full implication of his reply struck her, she grew furious.

"Wait just a minute. Is that what that scene at Wies was all about? Just a warm-up for a romantic little night together on the road? Well, Mr. Wainwright, if you think I'm going along with that, you're crazier than I thought. Now just get out of here."

"Sorry," he said, not budging from the middle of the room, where he now stood with his arms folded across his chest, looking like some angry feudal lord protecting his domain.

"Well, then, I will leave," Melody said heatedly, picking up her things and storming out the door. At the top of the steps she turned back, and her look was filled with hate.

"You're despicable, you know that."

Still calm in the face of her fury, he said, "You know, Miss Adamson, for a young lady's who's so determined to be liberated, you have some rather old-fashioned notions about sex."

With that Melody turned and ran down the steps, her eyes filled with tears. "Damn him! He is the most hateful man I have ever met," she raged, not noticing the startled gazes of the guests she passed on the stairs.

Four

It was very nearly dark and the mountains were merely purple blotches on the horizon, when Melody looked up and saw Brad striding toward her across the field. Turning her back on him, she watched the last streaks of pink fade from the sky. She had been standing here for the last hour or more, trying to swallow her pride and return to the hotel.

"Aren't you getting cold?" Brad asked at her side, holding out a jacket for her.

She shook her head and ignored the jacket, defiantly refusing to face him. Unfortunately, just at that moment she shivered uncontrollably in the cool spring air.

"Don't be a bloody little fool," he muttered in exasperation. "Put this on before you catch pneumonia."

She took the jacket finally, all the while managing to avoid looking into his eyes, which she was sure would be cold and accusing.

"I don't suppose you stopped by the desk on your way out here?" he asked casually, repeating the question when she didn't respond.

"Yes," she said then in a small voice.

"And did they tell you that there were no other rooms available for tonight? That we were lucky to get this one?"

"Yes."

"Did they also mention that there would be guests checking out tomorrow and that we would have the first available room?"

"Yes. They told me," she admitted reluctantly.

"Then why in God's name didn't you come back?" She realized the question was asked with more curiosity than anger.

"Because I felt like a bloody little fool, to use your expression."

"I rather thought you might," he said with a certain amount of smug satisfaction.

"Well, blast it all, you might have told me all of that yourself," she retorted sharply.

"Would you have listened? I had the impression you considered me something less than trustworthy."

She hesitated briefly, then shook her head. "You're right. I probably wouldn't have believed you."

"Look. I am sorry. I should have explained earlier, when I first called from Munich, but they promised to keep trying for another room. I'd hoped by the time we arrived the problem would be resolved. Okay?"

"Okay."

"Now, then, look at me," he said, insisting that she return his gaze. "I just want you to know that, contrary to what you seemed to think, the room arrangement had absolutely nothing to do with what happened back at Wies. You must believe that."

Melody studied him closely, trying to gauge the sincerity of his words. Before she could speak, he continued.

"If it will make you feel any better, I will spend the night on the sofa or the floor. That's really what I intended all along. Despite what happened this afternoon, I promised myself an uncomplicated trip and I intend to keep that promise. Sleeping in the same bed with you, no matter how innocent my intentions, would go a long way toward blowing that promise sky-high."

His eyes raked over her body suggestively, igniting a spark between them that lent truth to his words. A warm glow, caused partly by embarrassment and partly, Melody was forced to admit, by desire, swept over her in response to the sensuousness of his look.

"So, how about it?" he asked then, giving her his most appealing grin. "Trust me enough to come back now?"

"All right," she agreed, taking his outstretched hand and walking back indoors.

Once inside, she started toward the desk to retrieve her bags, but Brad halted her. "It's already taken care of."

She smiled. "Pretty sure of yourself, weren't you?"

"Pretty sure," he agreed complacently. "How about some dinner?"

He led her into the small, cheerful dining room, which was warmed by a blazing fire on the stone hearth and lit by candles on each table. It was a charming and romantic setting, and Melody wished she were sharing it with someone she loved, rather than this impossible, unpredictable man.

The menu had the usual assortment of plain, heavy food, including the ever-present Wiener schnitzel, which was rapidly becoming Melody's favorite German dish. She ordered it now and found the veal to be mouth-wateringly tender and the accompanying potatoes to be crispy and relatively nongreasy.

With mock seriousness, spurred by her outburst on the plane earlier in the day, Brad asked her permission to order a carafe of the local wine, a dry, white wine that Melody thought was wonderful. Not that she knew all that much about wine. One of those $150 bottles of rare vintage wine would be wasted on her. Her palate and her budget were used to the inexpensive California and New York wines back home.

Between the warmth of the room and the wine, Melody soon felt herself floating on a cloud of exhaustion. Her eyelids kept fluttering closed involuntarily, and she wasn't at all sure she'd be able to stay awake through dessert, much less dredge up enough energy to climb the stairs to their room. Not wanting to appear rude, she tried to stifle a yawn, then giggled when she noticed Brad doing the same thing.

"I think I've had it," she admitted. "It's been a very long day. For some reason I didn't get too much sleep last night."

"Neither did I," he reminded her, responding to her teasing tone. "I'll settle up with the waiter and we can get out of here. I can't recall when I've been more ready for bed."

At Melody's sharp intake of breath, he laughed. "Don't panic, my dear. I remember my promise."

Despite that promise, upstairs Melody was struck by a sudden shyness. She stood immobile in the middle of the room, trying to decide what she should do next. Sensing her nervousness, Brad suggested, "Go ahead and use the bathroom first. I think I'll go out for a walk."

"A walk," Melody said in astonishment. "I thought you were tired."

"I am, but a walk will help me to relax, especially after that heavy dinner. Go on. Get ready for bed before you collapse. If I'm not back by the time you go to sleep, I'll see you in the morning."

He left the room then, without coming near her, though Melody secretly wished he'd at least kissed her good night. When she'd finished her bath, he still had not returned, and, with a curious sense of disappointment, she climbed into the huge double bed alone. She wanted to stay awake until he came in, but within minutes she was pulled into a deep, dreamless sleep.

When she awoke, sunlight was streaming into the room and Brad was tossing restlessly on the sofa, his feet extending awkwardly over the end. He looked so uncomfortable, Melody felt guilty, thinking of her own uncramped night's sleep on the deep, soft mattress. As she studied Brad's face, an incredible feeling of tenderness swept through her. She was still watching him, when suddenly his eyes opened. He blinked and shook his head, as though to clear it.

"What kind of vision is this?" he asked groggily, as he noted the halo effect created by the sun striking her curly hair with its blond highlights. "I must be dreaming."

"Nope. I'm real enough," she said lightly.

"Come here and prove it," he dared softly.

"Not a chance," she said, scurrying into the bathroom as the sound of his laughter followed her. Feeling almost giddy with joy, she hummed snatches of "The Sound of Music," as she showered and dressed. Fluffing her hair dry with a towel, she noticed an uncommonly rosy glow in her cheeks and a sparkle in her eyes. She winked at her reflection in the mirror, then giggled.

"What's so funny?" Brad's voice, still husky with sleep, caused her to whirl around.

"Don't you believe in knocking?" she demanded, her voice filled with exasperation.

"You look lovely," he said, his gaze taking a lazy survey of her from head to toe.

"Don't try to change the subject, Mr. Wainwright. You are intruding on my privacy. Why, I could have been . . ."

"Naked," he teased, laughing as she blushed furiously.

"Oh, just get out of here," she snapped, throwing her brush at him. It barely missed him, as it sailed into the bedroom. He grinned and closed the door.

"Blast him," she muttered under her breath, irritated that he had such an uncanny knack for making her feel awkward and schoolgirlish.

When she finally emerged from the bathroom a few minutes later, she had managed to regain her composure, but her attitude was wary.

She needn't have worried. Brad was all business, as he outlined the day's schedule, then suggested she go down to breakfast.

Trying to match his indifferent tone, she said, "Fine. Shall I order something for you? Coffee? Tea?"

"Coffee and a couple of eggs would be great. I'll be right down."

In the dining room, while she waited for their order to arrive, Melody tried to figure out why Brad's sudden switch to a casual, distant manner should bother her even more than his suggestive banter.

She had almost no time to ponder the question, however. Brad and the waiter arrived almost simultaneously, and she was forced to put the issue aside. Through sheer determination she was able to establish a feeling of easygoing camaraderie during breakfast, and, as the day wore on, it became even easier. She had a natural curiosity about their two destinations, castles that had belonged to the Bavarian King Ludwig II, who had reigned in the nineteenth century.

They went to Linderhof first. With its spectacular fountain and its blue grotto, it was a charming miniature. With only a handful of rooms, it was the royal equivalent of a country cottage, intimate and cozy.

But if Linderhof was tiny in size, King Ludwig had hardly stinted on the interior. The ornateness of the Rococo decor kept Melody busy all morning, as she tried to find ways to photograph the perfection of the details. She was taking both black-and-white and color shots, which meant duplicated efforts. Some things lent themselves naturally to one or the other, but many of the interior shots particularly had to be done in both, so the magazine could determine later how it wished to use them.

By the time they left, Melody was exhausted but exhilarated. Her spirits climbed even more as they approached the second castle, Neuschwanstein. If Linderhof had charmed because of its size, then this one delighted because of the sheer audacity of its architecture. Sitting at the top of a mountain, its spires lifted toward the heavens like some childish fantasy castle, it could have been transported directly to Disneyland and fitted right in.

"It's incredible," Melody said, clapping her hands in glee as she caught her first glimpse of the palace.

When Brad had parked the car, he suggested they take a tram up to the castle itself, but Melody, spotting an innocent-looking trail, insisted they walk.

"You're sure?" Brad asked doubtfully.

"Of course. Come on. Look at all those people walking. It'll be fun. Unless, of course, you're not up to it," she challenged.

As the path went farther into the woods, it began to rise steeply. Although the afternoon was clear and cool, Melody found herself perspiring and panting as she struggled to keep pace with Brad's long-legged strides.

"Hey, slow down, will you," she pleaded breathlessly.

"Oh, sorry. Am I going too fast?" he asked innocently, turning away so she wouldn't see his grin.

"You know you are, you rat. Why didn't you warn me about this death march?"

"I tried to, but you insisted it looked like a perfect stroll. Far be it from me to disappoint a lady so clearly intent on taking an afternoon constitutional."

Still grinning, he trudged on. After another hundred yards, he slowed down. "We can stop up ahead, if you like, and have some lunch. There's a little restaurant for the fainthearted who can't take the climb all at once."

"Sounds wonderful," she agreed at once, refusing to acknowledge his look of amusement at her obvious relief.

Her happiness was short-lived, however, once she realized that there really was a long walk still ahead of them and it was all uphill as well.

"Isn't there some way to catch the tram from here?" she suggested casually.

"Nope. But you can make it. It's not that much farther."

Melody was determined not to beg for mercy again. As soon as they had finished their sandwiches and beer, they set out. At the top, while Brad made arrangements for them to go inside and take the photographs they needed, she sank down on a nearby boulder and tried to catch her breath. She was just beginning to think she might survive after all, when Brad returned with a guide. The guide escorted them inside, where, to Melody's absolute horror, she discovered hundreds of steps leading up through a tower into the castle itself.

"If we ever get out of here again," she muttered to Brad in an undertone, "I promise you I will get even with you for this."

His booming laugh echoed off the stone walls, causing Melody to give him a murderous look.

Hours later, as they drove back to Ettal through the gathering dusk, she was finally able to laugh, albeit feebly, at the afternoon's adventure. Even so, she refused to let Brad off the hook easily. "You owe me for this, Mr. Wainwright."

"Okay. I promise you a fine dinner, lots of soothing wine, and a gooey dessert guaranteed to add five pounds to that skinny little body of yours."

"It's a deal."

The day's congenial banter had enveloped Melody in a contented glow, which lasted until they walked into the lobby of the inn, where a stunning brunette, wearing a simple but revealing designer dress in blue silk was waiting. Melody immediately felt like a sloppy teenager in her informal jeans, and her reaction was intensified when she realized the woman was waiting for Brad.

"Darling," the woman greeted Brad in a well-modulated voice. "I've been waiting for you forever. Where on earth have you been?"

"Working," Brad said, his voice tight with exasperation. "I wasn't expecting you."

"I know you weren't. I finished my assignment early, checked with your office, and found out where you were and decided to come surprise you. I know how dreary it can be working out in the hinterlands all alone."

"I hardly think of this area as dreary," he snapped back with feeling. "And, as you can see, I am hardly alone."

He gestured toward Melody, who had been trying to slip away unnoticed. The woman, whom Melody had finally recognized as Lesley MacDonald, barely gave her a glance before going on.

"Well, aren't you the least little bit pleased to see me all the same?" she asked petulantly. "Come on, now, darling, take me to dinner and tell me all about what you're doing."

"I've already promised Melody a dinner in return for the strenuous day we've had. But you're welcome to join us, of course," he added reluctantly.

Overhearing him, Melody interrupted. "Hey, Brad, it's okay. I'm wiped out anyway. I'll just arrange to take a sandwich to my room or something. You go ahead and have dinner with your friend."

Lesley beamed. "See there, darling. I knew your little associate there wouldn't mind. Now come along," she said, placing a possessive hand on his arm and leading him to the dining room.

Melody, fighting back tears of exhaustion as much as of frustration, stumbled up the stairs, determined not to give either of them the satisfaction of watching them go off together. Because of this determination not to reveal her hurt, she did not see the fleeting look of longing on Brad's face as he looked after her. Nor did she hear the anger in his voice as he lashed out at his beautiful and desirable, but clearly unwanted, companion.

In her room, from which Brad's possessions had been removed during the day, she threw herself onto the bed and sobbed, racked with jealousy and an unexplained pain.

Suddenly she sat up, her puffy, tear-stained eyes wide with astonishment. Taking great gulps of air, she muttered aloud, "My gosh, I'm falling in love with the man."

Startled by the admission, she tried valiantly to deny it. Like a college debater, she argued with herself that what she was feeling was no more than an incredible physical chemistry, unlike any she had known with any other man. But she knew it was more than that, more than just a spark that seemed to ignite a burning desire in her veins with even the most casual contact.

Bradley Wainwright was exciting. He stirred not only her senses but her mind. She'd noticed that today, how she'd reached into herself for knowledge long left dormant. She would always have to be on her toes with him and she loved it. She loved it that he was so strong, yet able to reveal his sensitivity. She could even put up with his domineering attitude, if only a little of the gentleness that appeared in his writing would be directed toward her.

For a moment she allowed herself to revel in

this first tremulous stirring of love. She dreamed of what it would be like to share her life with this man, working with him as an equal, loving him as a partner in marriage. And then, she remembered Lesley MacDonald and the possessive way in which she'd taken over Brad's attention.

Ruefully, Melody realized her tiny, elfin-like body would be no competition for Lesley's tall, voluptuous beauty. Nor did she have the older woman's self-assurance, her sophistication. With these thoughts tumbling around in her head, Melody tossed and turned, tormented by images of Brad and Lesley together in each other's arms.

Five

Melody finally fell into a restless slumber just as streaks of grey began to lighten the morning sky. Asleep barely an hour, she reacted slowly and groggily when the pounding on her door began.

Muttering to herself as she tried to untangle the belt of her robe, which she'd left in a heap on the floor during the night, she stumbled to the door and called out, "Who is it?"

"It's me. Brad."

"Brad? What do you want?"

"I want you to open the door and let me in for starters," he ordered sharply.

Instinctively reacting to his tone, she started to unlatch the door, before remembering how she must look after her virtually sleepless night.

"You'll have to wait just a minute, Brad," she said, ignoring the angry outburst that followed, while she ran into the bathroom to splash cold water on her face and comb her tear-dampened hair.

A touch of lipstick and powdered blusher were unable to conceal the paleness of her skin, but it would have to do, she decided with a shrug.

As it turned out, she needn't have worried about the impression she would make. Brad barely looked at her, as he walked directly to the bed and sat down on the rumpled covers. Although his impatience at having been kept out in the hall seemed to be forgotten, he was clearly troubled about something.

"What time is it?" she asked, thinking perhaps she'd missed an arranged meeting. "Am I late?"

"No. No. You're not late. It's only seven o'clock. Look, Melody, I'd like to go back over to Wies today and I'd like to get started now. How fast do you suppose you can get ready?"

"In about fifteen minutes," Melody said, trying to conceal her puzzlement. "Is that okay?" she asked finally, when he continued to say nothing.

"Yeah. That'll be fine. I'll go downstairs and get some coffee and rolls to take along, so we won't have to waste time on breakfast. Is that all right with you?"

"Sure."

Running his hands through his hair with an air of complete distraction, he continued to sit on the bed as though searching for the right words for what he wanted to say.

Unable to stand his obvious dejection any longer, Melody asked softly, "Brad, is there something wrong?"

"What? No. No, there's nothing wrong." He

moved toward the door. "I'll meet you at the car in a few minutes."

Melody had no time to waste wondering what had put Brad into this strange, withdrawn mood. She showered, pulled on yet another pair of jeans and a dark green sweater, then swept her hair into two short ponytails that made her look about fifteen, instead of twenty-two. It wasn't exactly the look of sophistication she'd need to keep up with Lesley MacDonald, but Brad seemed unlikely to notice if she wore a gunnysack today.

At the thought of returning to Wies, alone with Brad, her gloomy mood of the night before lightened considerably, and her heart gave a little lurch at the thought of a repetition of the embrace they had shared there. Her spirits were climbing as she walked through the lobby of the inn, but they took a plunge as she heard a commanding female voice calling after her.

She turned and saw Lesley MacDonald striding purposefully toward her.

"Good morning," the older woman said brightly. "It's Miss Adamson, isn't it?"

"Yes. How are you, Miss MacDonald?"

"Fine. I'm looking for Brad. Do you have any idea where he might be? When I woke up this morning, he had already gone."

Melody's hands clenched involuntarily at her sides at the woman's words, but she managed to keep her voice even.

"Brad and I are just leaving. We have some work to do today. He's waiting for me now in the parking lot."

"Oh, how wonderful that I've caught you, then. I did so want to go along today, but Brad probably thought that I'd rather sleep in after our late night."

Her voice was honeyed lightness, but Melody noted an edge of steely determination there that made her feel a certain amount of pity for Brad.

Giving in to the inevitable, Melody led the way across the parking lot to the car, where Brad was waiting, slumped down behind the steering wheel. Seeing the two of them, he climbed out reluctantly. Before he could speak, however, Lesley had swept up to him and kissed him ardently, ignoring the tightness around his mouth, which Melody already recognized as a sign of barely controlled anger.

"Good morning, darling. I was so afraid I'd missed you this morning and I was really looking forward to our outing."

"Lesley, this is not an outing, as you call it," Brad began patiently. "It's work. Melody and I will have a lot to do today. I think it might be better if you just stayed here."

Melody, who knew full well that most of Brad's work on the assignment was already completed and that she could do hers on her own, was startled by his obvious desire to leave Lesley behind. The correspondent, however, either failed to understand or chose to ignore his words of dismissal.

"Oh, I know how fussy you are, darling. I promise I won't get in your way. I won't even suggest what approach you should take in your article, if that's what's worrying you," she said sweetly, as she climbed gracefully into the front seat, leaving Melody to squeeze into the tiny backseat.

Brad, aware that any further argument would be useless, gestured helplessly to Melody, climbed into the driver's seat, and started on the drive to Wies. The tension over the next few kilometers was so thick it seemed to lie over Melody and Brad at least like a heavy layer of fog.

Lesley, on the other hand, was apparently oblivious to it. She chattered away brightly, until Melody thought she would scream. By the time they arrived at the pilgrimage church, she was so anxious to escape the cloying atmosphere of the car that she grabbed up her cameras and practically ran on ahead.

"Let Brad fend for himself," she thought darkly, as she tried to focus her concentration on the photographic task ahead. And despite the morning's inauspicious beginning, she was soon lost in her work, fascinated with the play of light in the church and with Zimmermann's delicate, caring detail.

Hours later, physically drained but emotionally elated, she sensed someone standing quietly nearby. Looking up, she caught Brad watching her.

"Am I interrupting something crucial?" he asked.

"Nope. Nothing that can't wait for a little while. I can use a break," she said, wearily brushing escaping tendrils of hair from her flushed face.

"I'll bet you can. Do you realize you've been at

it for nearly five hours? It's way past lunch-
time.''

As though to confirm this, Melody's stomach
suddenly rumbled in complaint. Laughing, she
noted, ''Well, a part of me is apparently well
aware of that fact.''

''You keep working like this and I just may
have to revise my earlier impression of your level
of dedication to your profession.''

Melody looked at him sharply, searching for
any hint of sarcasm. Finding none, she decided to
leave well enough alone and change the subject.

''Where's Lesley?'' she asked in what she
hoped was an offhanded manner.

''In the car. Sulking.''

''Oh. About what?''

''The fact that it's hot. The fact that she snag-
ged her hose on a thorn. The fact that she's hungry. And thirsty.''

''Is that all?'' Melody asked innocently, trying
to hide a smile of satisfaction at the woman's ap-
parent discomfort.

''With Lesley that's more than enough. Any
one of the above would normally be cause for a
storm about the injustice of the gods or mankind
in general or me in particular.''

''You seem singularly unimpressed,'' she said
with some surprise.

''I'm used to it,'' Brad replied with a shrug.

''That must make her even angrier,'' Melody
suggested.

''As a matter of fact, it does,'' he said, grinning
for the first time that day. ''It makes her furious.''

"Well, it's all well and good if you're willing to let her unleash her fury in your direction, but I'd prefer to stay safely out of her path. She seems a bit intimidating to me."

"Lesley? Intimidating?" He sounded slightly incredulous. "You mean the poised lady-of-the-world manner?"

"That and the fact that she's very beautiful and very successful."

Brad's look was searching. "You're really serious, aren't you?"

Flustered by the intensity of his gaze, Melody tried to look away, but Brad gently grasped her chin and forced her to meet his eyes. "Listen, Melody, don't ever let anyone intimidate you, particularly Lesley. A lot of that beauty you mention is manufactured and not very deep. As for the success, I've told you I think your work is very good. Someday you'll have all the success and recognition you want. Just don't let it spoil your gentle spirit. And remember this . . . Lesley has her own demons to fight."

He leaned down then and kissed her, a tender, fleeting kiss that was over in an instant, though not before it had stirred Melody's senses.

"Come on, half-pint. We'd better go feed the famous correspondent, before her network sues us for damaging their property. They like their journalists thin, but not haggard and emaciated."

The drive back to Ettal was only slightly better than the morning's ride. Undercurrents of tension still filled the car, but Lesley was silent and Melody was able to watch the passing scenery with increasing delight. The splashes of color, the distant, snowcapped mountain peaks, the grazing sheep all combined for a pastoral scene of heart-wrenching beauty.

Back at the inn Brad immediately announced his intention of spending the afternoon working on his article in his room. "Alone," he emphasized with a pointed look at Lesley, who promptly stormed off toward the dining room in a huff.

"Subtlety is not one of your strong points, is it?" Melody commented, as she watched Lesley's angry departure.

"With Lesley subtlety doesn't work. Now then, what are you going to do for what's left of the day?"

"If you don't need the car, I thought I might drive over to Oberammergau and do some shopping. Would that be all right?"

"Of course. There are some wonderful shops for wood carvings over there. And be sure to take your camera. Even though it's not going to be part of the article, Oberammergau has some fantastic picture possibilities you won't want to miss."

"What do you mean?" Melody asked, watching the familiar gleam of excitement begin to shine once more in Brad's eyes.

"Never mind," he teased. "Let it be a surprise."

"But if you don't tell me what to look for, how will I know when I find it?" she asked reasonably. Brad laughed at her look of confusion. "Trust me. You'll know. Now run along and have a good time. Don't worry about getting back at any special time. I won't be needing the car again today.

I'm going to have an early dinner in my room and get some sleep. Last night and this morning have worn me out."

Melody, her cheeks flaming at the implication of his words, had no doubt he was referring to Lesley. Again images of the two of them together making love flashed into her mind. While the torment of those images had robbed her of a night's sleep, the reality of it had obviously tired Brad as well.

Taking the car keys from Brad, Melody escaped quickly, before he could see the effect of his words. She was determined, particularly now that his lover was very much in the picture, that he not discover how vulnerable she was to him, how much she loved him.

The drive to Oberammergau took little more than half an hour, and Melody's mood began to lift the minute she started through the narrow, winding streets. She knew immediately what Brad had meant about the town, as she passed house after house with storybook scenes painted on their stucco sides. Pastel now with age, many of the scenes reminded her of childhood fairy tales, bringing a smile to her lips.

Although the village was tiny, with barely 5,000 residents, its fame was worldwide, thanks to its Passion Play, presented only every ten years, and attended by hundreds of thousands of visitors from around the globe. The city was jammed during the months of the presentations, but now it was just a sleepy little community in the foothills of the Alps.

Melody wandered from shop to shop, admiring

the brightly painted souvenirs so typical of Bavaria. She found a tray of carved wooden egg holders that would be perfect for Aunt Leah, whose boiled egg and toast were a morning ritual.

By now it was dusk, and she was debating returning to Ettal, when her rumbling stomach reminded her that, in all of the tension of the afternoon, she had skipped lunch entirely. The prospect of a lonely meal at the inn or, worse yet, a strained meal with Brad and Lesley did not appeal to her at all.

As she walked slowly and dejectedly back to the car, she passed a small, cozy-looking restaurant and impulsively decided to stay in Oberammergau for dinner.

Inside, she knew at once it had been a good decision. The atmosphere was friendly, with locals calling greetings between tables and boisterous laughter filling the air. A beaming host, speaking halting English, led her to a table near a blazing fire. Although it had been warm during the day, the temperature had fallen sharply with the onset of dusk, and Melody was glad of the warmth from the nearby hearth.

When she had placed her order, she sat back, sipping slowly from a glass of wine as she watched the other diners, enjoying their easy camaraderie, even though she could understand only a smattering of what was being said around her. Her dinner, when it came, was perfect, the sausages spicy and satisfying. She was finishing her glass of wine, when she realized that several young people at a neighboring table were gazing speculatively in her direction. One of them, a tall, handsome blond with the body and winter tan of a skier, caught her eye and smiled. When she returned the smile, he came over to her table.

"You're American." It was a statement, rather than a question.

"Yes. From New York."

"You are here alone?"

Years of cautiousness made Melody momentarily uneasy, despite the friendliness of the young man's gaze. After hesitating for a moment, she replied slowly, "Tonight, yes. But I'm working near here with a friend. He's at the inn in Ettal."

"A pretty lady should not be left alone . . . ever," he said seriously, causing Melody to blush. "Would you like to join us? My friends would love to practice their English, and I would like to escort a beautiful woman for an evening."

"I'd love to join you," she said, her earlier restraint forgotten. She was flattered, too, by the look of sheer delight on his face at her response.

When she had been introduced to the others, they insisted she try the local beer. "You must have a stein of beer for when the singing begins," they explained.

"Singing?"

"Oh, yes," enthused a slightly plump girl of about eighteen, her golden hair in braids, which had been looped into circles over each ear. "In a little while there will be a little band and a singer and we will all join in. The Germans love to sing."

"And to drink," Melody's companion added wryly.

He had introduced himself as Hans Brinkerhof, and, as Melody had suspected from his lithe, muscular body, he was a skier. He had been on the German skiing team, participated in the Winter Olympics, and had competed around the world. Now he was an instructor at a nearby resort.

"Is that how you learned to speak English so well?" Melody asked.

"No, though it gave me the opportunity to use what I had learned. In Germany all students study more than one language. I was taught English and French. I am not completely fluent in all of them, but I can get along okay."

"I wish I had learned other languages when I was young," Melody said with a sigh. "In America it is not required to be fluent in other languages, and I'm finding it much more difficult to pick them up now that I'm older. I can get by, if I need to order a meal or find the train station or get a hotel room. But heaven help me if I ever need anything any more complicated."

Suddenly, as they were talking, the promised music began and conversation was drowned out by the communal sing-along. Beer steins waved in the air, as the crowd enthusiastically sang the words of a drinking song that was obviously a favorite. With Hans whispering the words in her ear, Melody tried to join in, and the others laughed as they heard her awkward pronunciation. Still, at the song's end they cheered her efforts. As the boisterous music went on and on, Melody fell under the spell of the friendliness, the beer, and the warmth in Hans's eyes as he coached her.

When she finally looked at her watch, it was

nearly midnight and, though Brad had said they wouldn't be working again in the morning, she was appalled at how the time had slipped away.

"I must get back to Ettal," she told the disappointed Hans.

"I will walk with you to your car, then," he said, rising with her as she circled the table saying her farewells to his friends. When she asked about her share of the bill for the evening, he dismissed it. "That is not for you to worry about. I will take care of it."

"But, Hans, that is not necessary."

"It is my wish," he said with finality.

As they strolled to the car, Melody gazed up at the stars, which seemed so much brighter here than back home, where they competed with neon and street lights in the night sky. To Hans she said, "Thank you for a wonderful evening. It has been very special for me."

"For me too, my Melody," he said, looking into her upturned face. "You are very beautiful," he added softly, his lips brushing gently across her forehead. "I would like to see you again. Will you be here long?"

"Only a few more days, I think."

"Then I must make the most of the time that is left. Are you free tomorrow?"

"I'm not really sure. I know we're not working in the morning, but Brad hasn't mentioned anything yet about the afternoon."

"Then I will come and join you for breakfast. We can plan the rest of the day then. That is okay, yes?"

Melody was reluctant to make a commitment,

but Hans looked at her so earnestly she couldn't possibly refuse him. She worried, though, about pursuing the relationship, when, despite Hans's admiring attention it had been Brad's dark, brooding face in her thoughts all evening.

"That's ridiculous," she thought, shaking herself mentally. "Brad has Lesley. There is no reason I shouldn't see Hans."

Aloud she said finally, "Fine. You come over in the morning. I should be able to find out by nine what our schedule will be."

Hans squeezed her heartily. "That is wonderful. I will see you in the morning. Are you sure you would not like me to drive you back now? These roads can be confusing, if you are not familiar with them."

"Don't worry about me. I'm sure I'll be just fine."

An hour later, thoroughly lost after taking a wrong turn, she remembered those words. Her mind, tumbling around with images of Brad and Lesley and concern about her own actions in leading Hans on, had not been on her driving, and she had turned right, instead of left, at a crossroad just outside of Oberammergau. At least that's what she thought she had done.

Finally, near tears, she pulled to the side of the road.

Her gloved hands grasping the wheel tightly, she tried to force herself to concentrate. "All I have to do is remember when I made the wrong turn and what I've done since then," she said, trying to calm herself. She could not recall having passed any road markers for at least a half hour. Not had there been lights glimmering from any farmhouses.

By now she was shaking. Although she knew she was in no real danger, she was cold and tired. Still, she knew it was pointless to keep wandering around in the dark. Who knew where she would wind up then?

It was some time later, she wasn't sure how long, when the sound of a motor startled her from her reverie. Lights were approaching from a distance.

Melody climbed out to stand beside her car, after turning on her own headlights to attract attention. Waving frantically, she flagged down the other driver, a farmer with a truckload of produce heading for the market.

Greeting him in halting German, she tried to explain her plight, but the man looked increasingly puzzled as she talked in a mixture of German and English. Growing more and more frustrated with each passing moment, Melody suddenly burst into tears. The farmer, understanding that she was apparently lost and in distress, pointed to her car, apparently asking if it was broken.

"No. No. The car is fine. I just need to get back on the right road to Ettal," she said, wiping at her tears.

Then, with a sudden flash of inspiration, she recalled that there was a map in the car's glove compartment. Running over to the car, she rummaged around until she found it, then took it back to the farmer and pointed to Ettal.

"Ja. Ettal," the man said, beaming with sudden understanding. Pointing to the map, he was able to explain to her where she was and how she could get back on the correct route.

Thanking the man profusely, she offered him a tip for his help, but he waved it away. Bowing to her, he climbed back into his truck, waited for her to start off in the right direction, then tooted his horn and went on his way.

Back at the inn, weak with exhaustion, she nearly stumbled as she entered the lobby, where she found Brad pacing like a caged lion.

"Brad," she called out, her voice filled with surprise.

Spotting her, his face broke into a glowing smile of relief, the tension in his body seeming to ebb away before her eyes. Gathering her into his arms, he muttered roughly, "Thank God, you're all right. I've been worried sick about you."

"About me?"

"Yes, you little goose. Do you realize it is nearly four A.M. and that you've been gone for hours? I expected you back by dinnertime."

"I thought you would be asleep. You said you were going to bed early."

"Well, I didn't. I called your room about seven to see if you'd like to have dinner. I called again at eight and at nine. By then I was frantic. My God, Melody, don't ever do this to me again."

All the while, as he talked, Brad was holding her tightly, as though he was afraid to let her go again. His hands caressed her gently, like a fragile doll. But the sensations being aroused in Melody were hardly doll-like. Liquid heat was coursing through her veins at his touch. Just when she would have molded her body more closely to his and given in to her feelings, a strident voice interrupted.

"You really have been most inconsiderate," Lesley said coldly. "The least you could have done was phone. Instead, you ruin our entire evening, while you're off gallivanting around the countryside."

Lesley's look was murderous, as she gave full vent to her anger. When she would have gone on, Brad intervened.

"Stop it, Lesley. We don't even know what happened."

"Well, I'm sure I know. Little Miss Innocent here probably picked herself up some local yokel and had a ball, while you sat here worrying yourself sick."

"I did meet some people in Oberammergau," Melody began defensively. "But for your information, for the last several hours I have been lost. I had to wait until a farmer came along to show me the way back to the inn. Now if you don't mind, Brad, I think I've had about all I can take for one night."

Slipping out of Brad's embrace, which he had not dropped throughout her heated exchange with Lesley, she stalked off toward the stairs. She could hear the journalist's sharp intake of breath and her complaints about the rudeness of "some people," but she was in no mood to care about any further insults. Nor was she up to any more of Brad's relentless questioning about her evening. Morning would be soon enough to face all that.

Six

Unable to sleep, despite or perhaps because of the night's events, Melody was up at the crack of dawn, restlessly pacing about her room.

"This is absurd," she muttered at last, grabbing her jacket and slipping quietly down the stairs to the deserted lobby.

Outside a morning mist shrouded the distant mountains and the air was damp and clean, as she set out toward the huge Ettal Abbey down the road. Built by Emperor Ludwig in 1330 and inhabited by Benedictine monks, the abbey had become an attraction for tourists. At this hour, though, it basked in a reverent silence and seemed to share its calm with Melody.

Soothed by the peaceful morning, she strolled back to the inn to find that it had come to life. She could smell the fresh bread baking in the kitchen and suddenly realized that she was ravenous.

The dining room was empty as she entered, but a beaming, young waitress materialized almost at once to lead her to a table by the windows, where she could look out on the fields of wild flowers. Moments later the waitress reappeared with a steaming pot of tea, a basket of bread still warm from the oven, creamy butter, and a bowl of strawberry jam.

Everything tasted so delicious, it was all Melody could do to resist the temptation to lick the sticky, sweet jam from her fingers. It seemed such a waste to wipe it off on her napkin.

"Penny for your thoughts, Miss Adamson," that familiar deep voice whispered provocatively in her ear.

"They're worth much more than that," she insisted with an injured expression, as she turned to gaze up at Brad, whose eyes caressed her.

Leaning down slowly, his eyes locked with hers, he kissed her gently. "What can I buy with a kiss, then?"

To herself Melody thought, "Almost anything," but aloud she managed to say tartly, "I'll have to check its value on the international market."

"I assure you it's very high," he responded with a wink, as he moved to sit opposite her. "By the way, what are you doing up at this hour? I thought you'd sleep till noon."

Melody shrugged. "What about you? You didn't get much sleep either."

"I guess we both had a lot on our minds. I had some decisions to make."

"About what?" she asked, then noticed the

closed expression on his face. "Or would you rather not talk about them?"

"Not yet. I don't think the timing's quite right," he said, giving her a searching look, filled with meaning.

The depth of that gaze made Melody uneasy, and she was forced to look away. "Perhaps you're right. About the timing, I mean," she said, unable to hide how flustered she had suddenly become.

As Melody tried to hide her nervousness, Hans's tall, blond figure loomed over their table.

"Melody, little one, I am interrupting something," he said, his look questioning.

Flushing even more under the intensity of his gaze and the sudden scowl that appeared on Brad's face, she stammered, "Hans . . . I didn't expect . . . I mean, it's so early."

"I could not wait to see you again. Would you like me to wait in the lobby, perhaps, until you finish your talk?"

"No. Of course not. Please, sit down. Hans, this is my boss, Bradley Wainwright. Brad, Hans Brinkerhof."

The two men shook hands warily, but with his naturally open and friendly nature, Hans recovered quickly.

"Herr Wainwright, I have read your articles, I believe. They are excellent. You have a gift for making a place come to life. I always long to visit the villages you describe."

"Thanks," Brad said, his previously frosty demeanor thawing ever so slightly.

"You are here to write about Bavaria?"

"Yes. I have done most of my research, but there are a few final details to complete, while Miss Adamson shoots the pictures."

"You are taking the pictures," Hans said to Melody, his voice filled with surprise.

Melody could not keep the edge of defensiveness from her voice as she replied, "What's so shocking about that?"

"Nothing, little one. Do not ruffle your feathers so. It is just that you did not mention last night that you are a photographer."

"Well, I am. And a good one at that," she snapped.

Brad's amusement was growing at this exchange.

"You'll have to excuse Melody. She has a quick temper, where her work is concerned. Too many men have apparently implied that she'd be better off in a kitchen, rather than a darkroom," he inserted smoothly, winking at Hans.

"But you hired her, so she must be good," Hans said.

As the conversation swirled around her, as though she weren't even there, Melody grew more and more resentful. She was about to make another angry retort, when Brad's next comment startled her into silence.

"She is good," he was telling Hans. "One of the best photographers I've ever used. Everything you say about my gift for words more than applies to Melody's talent with a camera. You must ask her to show you some of her work. The photographs are truly remarkable, particularly those of people. She manages somehow to capture on film more than a mere physical resemblance. She finds that one moment that reveals the soul."

Melody gaped at Brad. "I didn't know that you . . ." Her voice trailed off meekly.

"That I thought so highly of your work? Surely you know me well enough by now to realize that you would not be along on this assignment if you were not the best. I seem to recall that you assured me that you were, in fact. That ability alone overcame my resistance to your . . ."

"To my sex?"

At Hans's inquisitive glance, she added, "Brad is one of those who thinks women have no place leaving the confines of a home to do a so-called man's job."

Hans grinned. "I think, perhaps, I understand. In your case, anyway. It would be very difficult for a man to let someone so beautiful stray very far from his sight."

"Lovely sentiments, Hans, but I'm afraid anyone crazy enough to fall in love with Melody will have to be willing to give her a very free rein. She is an incredibly independent young woman. She's also very stubborn."

"I've had to be tenacious, Brad, and you are the perfect example of why, so don't you dare start . . ."

"Start what," he teased, lifting her hand and bringing it to his lips for a quick kiss.

Melody yanked her hand away, hoping he hadn't noticed how that slight contact had made her tremble. Judging from the deep-throated laugh that boomed forth, however, he was obviously very much aware of her susceptibility and was thoroughly enjoying her confusion.

As she was trying to regain her composure, Brad stood. "I must run along now. Hans, I hope you will take good care of Melody today. I have to drive back to Munich, which will take most of the day."

At Melody's look of surprise, he explained, "I have some business to take care of, and Lesley has a plane to catch."

Her initial dismay at Brad's announcement was tempered with relief at the thought of Lesley MacDonald's departure.

"We will be having a very busy day tomorrow, though, so don't stay out too late," Brad warned.

"I will see that she is back in plenty of time to get her rest," Hans promised, oblivious to the irritated expression that flickered across Melody's face.

The thought that these two men were so casually taking charge of her life, as though she were a mere child, exasperated her beyond words. She was about to lash out at Hans, once Brad was out of earshot, but a sudden doubt about her motives warned her to keep silent.

Perhaps it was the jovial camaraderie between the two that was truly the source of her irritation. Had she wanted them to behave as rivals, to demonstrate a sudden surge of jealousy at the idea of competing for her attention? Maybe so, she admitted to herself.

Well, she should have known better, Brad wasn't interested in her. Not really. A few sexual overtures meant nothing. As for Hans, he'd merely accepted Brad in the role in which she'd cast him: as her boss and nothing more. There was no reason for them not to get along, she reasoned.

And yet . . . and yet, she wished they hadn't, if she were to be perfectly honest about it. Or, more to the point, that Brad had been affected by seeing her with another attractive man.

"Melody? Little one? Why are you looking so cross?" Hans asked, his voice shaming her with its genuine sound of concern. She tried to smile, but it was a weak effort.

"Now you look sad. Well, never mind that, I will wipe that sadness from your eyes. We will have an adventure today. I will take you to the lodge where I work, and we can go for a long walk along the trails. Most of the snow is gone now, but the air is so fresh and clean and cool, it will make your lungs gasp with joy."

"That certainly sounds like an experience I owe my lungs," she responded, laughing at last. "Okay, let's get on with it. Shall I change?"

"You have on comfortable shoes for walking?" She nodded.

"Then you are fine as you are," he said, taking her hand, as he led her from the inn to his bright red sports car parked outside.

To Melody's amazement the car was surrounded by curious boys, although she could see nothing especially flashy or unique about it. In fact, it was one of those little gas-efficient models that one could see by the hundreds on every highway in Germany. As they approached the car, they were spotted by one of the youths.

"Hans," he shouted enthusiastically. "It's Hans Brinkerhof!"

His shouts alerted the others, and in an instant Melody and Hans were surrounded. Melody was lost as the conversation exploded around her in bursts of rapid-fire, excited German. Slipping through the crowd, she stood back to watch with a mixture of amusement and awe as Hans patiently answered all of their questions. Then, he, too, edged from their midst to help Melody into the car. The boys stood back politely, almost reverentially, to allow him to pass.

"What on earth was that all about?" Melody asked, when the waving boys were no longer in sight. "Is there something amazing about this car that I didn't notice? Or is it you?"

Hans seemed momentarily embarrassed. "They noticed the Olympic sticker on the car, that is all."

"And they recognized you. Of course. How could I have been so stupid? You're a celebrity."

"No," he insisted. "I'm not a celebrity, not in the American sense anyway. I have a small following, mainly among the youngsters in this area, who idolize Olympic athletes. To participate in the Olympics in my country is a great honor."

"Isn't it in all countries?" Melody asked, puzzled.

"Not so much in America, I think. In many countries, including Germany, the athletes are subsidized by the government in one way or another. They are official representatives, receiving a great deal of respect from the country's leaders.

National attention is focused on them, not just when they win, but all during their years of preparation.

"In your country, it seems to me, their acclaim comes only when they perform spectacularly, as your hockey team did against the Russians. For the others, their fame is fleeting, lasting only as long as their event appears before the television cameras."

Melody was thoughtful, as she considered Hans's analysis.

"I never thought about it that way before, but I suppose you are right. We don't seem to care about our Olympic athletes until they capture at least a gold medal or two. Then we give them contracts for commercials and turn them into television commentators."

Hans burst out laughing.

"What's so funny? It's true."

"I know it is. I was just thinking about how many Olympic stars from the past I met, when they interviewed me for American network TV. In my country they are more likely to wind up like me, teaching at a resort somewhere."

"That's probably a lot healthier."

"No doubt. But it's not as glamorous."

"I think it is. I've never met a handsome ski instructor before," Melody said, giving him a warm smile.

Hans reached over to clasp her hand in a gesture that was more romantic than friendly. The tenderness in his caress made Melody feel uncomfortable. She felt the first stirrings of uneasiness that Hans's attentions might become too serious too quickly. As though sensing something of her disquiet, Hans released her hand and began a casual description of the countryside through which they were passing.

The narrow, winding road they traveled twisted uphill. Although the sun had been shining brightly as they left Ettal, only glimpses of clear blue sky could be seen through the tall, dark green pines that towered on either side of the road, casting giant shadows over their route.

Hans made an entertaining guide, interspersing bits of local folklore with his travelogue. Melody eyed him skeptically during one of these tales.

Catching her look, he asked indignantly, "You do not believe me?"

"That sounds suspiciously like something from Hans Christian Andersen or Grimm's fairy tales," she chided him reproachfully.

"No, I swear to you, Melody. They say it is true."

"Who says so?"

"The people who live around here. They all say they have known someone who has seen such a creature living in these woods."

"Ah ha," she cried, as though catching him in an admission of clear guilt. "They have known someone who has seen it, but they've never seen it themselves, have they? Have they, Hans?"

He grinned sheepishly. "Perhaps not," he admitted. "But it makes a wonderful story, does it not?"

Melody chuckled. "A wonderful story," she agreed.

Moments later Hans turned into a driveway that was nearly hidden from view and drove slowly over the deeply rutted road.

"If this is the entrance to your resort, they must not care much about the damage they do to their guests' cars," Melody said, bouncing in her seat. "Or do they operate the local garage as well?"

"This is the back way in," Hans explained. "It is shorter and not so bad, if you drive slowly."

When they emerged at last in a clearing, Melody had to cover her mouth to keep from giggling aloud with childlike glee. Clearing her throat and rummaging in her purse for some undetermined item, she tried to avoid meeting Hans's gaze. He saw right through her.

"You find it amusing, little one?" he asked, trying to smother his own laughter.

"I'm sorry," she apologized. "It's just that it's so . . . so . . ."

"German," Hans supplied succinctly.

"Not exactly. It's like something from those fairy tales we were talking about earlier," she said, as she stared at the lodge with its brightly painted decorations and intricate carvings.

"I know. It reminds me of a gingerbread house. When I first saw it, I thought for sure Hansel and Gretel would be popping out any minute. Come. Let me show you around."

Inside, the lodge was decorated in similar storybook fashion. A blazing fire roared in the huge stone hearth, and antlered elk heads adorned the walls. A few couples were lounging around in the overstuffed chairs, talking and drinking tea or coffee from steaming mugs. Behind the desk a young man in dark green lederhosen and a matching vest with bright embroidery was frantically trying to soothe an irritated guest and man the phones at the same time. Despite the confusion, her managed to give them a friendly wave as they passed.

"That is Eric. He will be a fine skier by the end of next winter. Already he is the best in his amateur class. He is lucky to work here, where he can practice as much as he likes."

"He seems so young. Where is his family?"

"They run the lodge. And you are right. He is young, only fifteen."

"What about his education?"

"We are not quite so single-minded here that we neglect the basics, Melody," Hans said stiffly. "He goes to school. In fact, he skis the five miles to the schoolhouse every day."

"You're kidding."

"No, indeed. That is not so far," he assured her.

"It sounds like an incredibly long distance to me."

"Only because you are not used to it. Besides," he added with a grin, "it goes quickly when you are speeding down the side of a mountain."

"Down the mountain," Melody repeated, her voice still incredulous. "What about coming home? Up the mountain?"

"Ah, yes, that is the hard part," Hans replied with a wink. "But it makes one's legs very strong and that is necessary to become a great skier."

Their conversation was cut short as Hans led her into a huge, steamy kitchen, fragrant with the smell of baking pies and simmering soups.

Melody couldn't resist lifting the lid of one of the huge kettles and sniffing deeply as the aroma wafted up at her.

"It smells delicious," she said appreciatively.

"You like?" a friendly voice, thick with a German accent, asked from behind her.

Melody turned to face a heavyset woman, her face wreathed in a broad smile. "Oh, yes. What is it?"

"A goulash. Vegetables, beef, and lots of spices. Sit and I give you some."

Melody sought approval from Hans, who was nodding.

"You might as well sit, Melody. Once Marta makes up her mind to feed you, it's impossible to leave before you're stuffed. One look at your tiny body and I'm sure she won't let you get away until she's sure you won't die of malnutrition."

"Ach, you," Marta began scathingly. "You don't like my cooking so much, huh? Then you don't need to eat it. I feed your friend."

He quieted her with a hearty hug. "I love your food and you know it. Frau Krantz, this is Melody Adamson."

"You call me Marta, like Hans. You are an American?"

Melody nodded.

"You are staying here?"

"No. In Ettal. I'm a photographer and I'm on an assignment for a magazine."

"So, Hans, you find yourself someone beautiful and talented this time. Your taste is improving," Marta teased fondly. "Hers, I'm not so sure. Going out with a big one like you, maybe not so smart. You be careful of him, Fräulein. He is, what you call it, a ladies' man?"

"Don't you listen to her, Melody. She's just jealous because she's already married and can't have me for her own."

"You," she said, waving a soup ladle at him menacingly. "Seriously, though, he is a fine man, our Hans. I've know him since he was a boy."

All the while, as Marta chattered about Hans and his boyhood, she kept refilling Melody's soup bowl. A chunk of freshly baked bread was passed with each new ladleful of soup. After the third refill, Melody pushed her chair away from the table.

"No more," she pleaded. "I can't move now. I'm afraid I ate like a pig. It was fantastic. Will you tell me how to make it?"

"Of course," Marta agreed, with a pleased smile. "I go and write for you," she said, bustling from the kitchen.

"She's charming," Melody said, when Marta had gone.

"She's been like a mother to me, to all the children around here. She only had one child of her own and he died. I think we've all been substitutes for him. She never tires of listening to our problems, filling us up with good food and chastizing us, when we've gotten out of line. I've spent a lot of hours in this kitchen," he said, looking around him and lost, for the moment, in his memories.

When he spoke again, his voice was barely audible, and Melody sensed that tears were barely contained. "After my own mother died, Marta became even more important to me. I don't know what I would have done without her caring."

As though afraid of revealing too much about his childhood, Hans quickly changed the subject, but not before Melody caught a glimpse of the sensitive, lonely boy he had been. She could sympathize with his feeling of loss. It must have been much like her own.

Calling out to Marta, he pulled Melody from her chair.

"Come now, lazy one, we must walk off all of that food."

When Marta reappeared in the doorway, he said, "I'm going to take Melody on a hike. Maybe up to the old cabin."

Marta looked surprised, but only nodded. "You come back before you leave?"

"Of course. Have some hot chocolate ready for us, okay?"

"You want hot chocolate, you make it yourself," Marta said with a haughty sniff, belied by the twinkle in her eyes. "I am not your personal cook, young man. I have a whole dining room full of guests to feed."

"Okay. Okay," Hans said, throwing up his hands in a gesture of surrender. "See you later."

Outside the air was just as crisp and clean as Hans had promised, and Melody breathed deeply, inhaling the fresh pine scent. The trail sloped gently up through the woods, and she had no trouble keeping pace with Hans, who seemed content to stroll along in companionable silence.

Following along the bank of a burbling little

stream, they eventually came upon a clearing. A small cabin sat at the far edge, its sagging porch and overgrown lawn a silent rebuke to those who had abandoned it. An odd, faraway look came into Hans's eyes, a look that disturbed Melody.

"Hans," she said, touching his arm. "Perhaps we should go back?"

He looked down at her, a sad smile lifting the corners of his mouth, but not quite reaching his eyes.

"It's okay, little one."

"But you look so unhappy."

"I am just remembering the way it was. This was where I lived as a boy. I haven't been back in a long time. It was too painful. And," he added, pausing significantly, "I have never brought anyone here before."

Suddenly Melody realized why Marta had seemed so surprised when Hans had indicated where they were going. She had assumed that Melody must be someone very special to be asked to share in a part of Hans's past that had remained tucked away for so long.

At last she was able to say with sincerity, "I'm glad you brought me. I think I understand what you must be feeling. I remember how difficult it was to see my home again, after my parents were killed. It seemed so empty and lifeless, as though it were mocking all the joy and laughter we had shared there.

"Finally I was able to accept that it was just a place, that it had no power of its own. Certainly, no matter how much it might change, it could never rob me of the memories of how it had been.''

Hans gave her a grateful squeeze. "You are very perceptive, little one."

Instead of releasing her, though, he pulled her more tightly into his arms. His kiss was a gentle, questioning one, and when Melody did not respond, he did not press her, though there was a look of hurt in his eyes.

"I'm sorry," she whispered, her face buried against the rough wool of his sweater.

Cupping her chin in his hand, Hans forced her to meet his eyes. Then, tracing her lips with the tips of his fingers he silenced her apology.

"Ssh. Quiet, little one. It is okay. You have nothing for which to apologize. I am the one. I am rushing you. It is just that our time is so short."

He sighed.

"Oh, well, I will find a way to make the most of our time. Perhaps I can even make you change your plans and stay longer. Now, come, let's go back and have that hot chocolate."

Melody was grateful for this reprieve, but she could not ignore the chill deep within her, as they returned to the lodge. Though there was a sharp bite to the air, she knew that the cold that seemed to encase her heart came from a sense of loss. Hans was clearly a very special man, and she regretted her inability to share his attraction. But he simply did not stir her senses as Brad did.

She was able to put aside her dismay temporarily as they visited briefly with Marta before leaving, but on the long drive back to Ettal, she had plenty of time to think. Reluctantly, she decided at last that there was only one thing to be done: She must tell Hans exactly how she felt. He deserved that much honesty from her. Perhaps then they could become friends at least.

She glanced over at the handsome profile beside her, resisting the urge to push back the blond hair that drooped over the smooth, tanned forehead. She studied the firm hand, with its squared-off, blunt fingers, which maintained a seemingly loose control of the steering wheel. As casual as that grip appeared, though, Melody could almost feel its mastery over the car and wondered briefly what it would be like to have that hand control her body, mastering its erogenous zones with the same sure touch.

She recalled having similar thoughts on the first ride with Brad, only days earlier. But now the thought was only momentarily titillating, no more urgent or demanding than the most casual cocktail party encounter with a stranger who radiated an undeniable virility. It was more curiosity than desire. Brad, on the other hand, inspired an unrelenting lust for fulfillment that shook the uninitiated Melody to her very core.

Blushing at the wanton turn her thoughts had taken, she was glad that it was dusk and that her face was masked by the gathering darkness. She forced her mind back on the task ahead of her. She would have preferred avoiding such a conversation with Hans, but that was not only unrealistic, it was unfair. He had to know where he stood with her.

As he turned the car smoothly into the inn's driveway, she spoke. "Thank you for a wonderful day. The lodge is terrific and Marta is really something special. It's no wonder you adore her."

"She liked you also. I could tell. She usually grumbles at any interruption in her routine, but she would have kept you there for the rest of the afternoon. I think she realizes how much you mean to me."

"Hans . . ." Melody began, pausing awkwardly. Taking a deep breath, she went on. "Hans, that's something I think we have to talk about. Can you come in for coffee?"

"I have the time for coffee, yes. But I have a feeling I am not going to like very well the conversation that comes with it. Is that so?"

"Perhaps not," she said honestly. "But there are some things I simply must say. It wouldn't be fair for me to keep silent."

"Then I will listen," Hans promised, helping her from the car and escorting her to the inn's dining room.

As Melody's eyes scanned the room, looking for a table, she spotted Brad, his back turned toward them. Hans saw him at the same moment.

"Isn't that Herr Wainwright? Perhaps we should speak to him before we have our talk."

Reluctantly, Melody followed Hans to Brad's table. As they drew nearer, she realized he was not alone. A small boy, a mirror image of the man, sat across from him, his dark eyes heavy with sleep, his black hair a mass of tousled curls. Melody's heart turned over at the sight of this miniature of the man she loved, and instantly she knew she was not prepared to hear anything about this child and his relationship to Brad.

"Herr Wainwright," Hans began, ignoring Melody's frantic tug on his arm. Brad looked up, smiling a welcome, and then it was too late.

"Melody, Hans," he greeted them enthusiastically, his glance holding an extra warmth as it fell on Melody. "How was your day? I'm glad you took my advice and returned early. Here, let me get a couple of chairs and you can join us."

For a moment Hans tried to demur, but Brad ignored his protests, quickly drawing up the extra chairs from a neighboring table. Melody sat down with a leaden feeling at the pit of her stomach, hoping desperately that her suspicions about the boy, who looked to be about five or six, would not be confirmed. Her hopes were dashed, however, the first time he spoke.

"Daddy," he said, his eyes now alert and dancing with mischief and excitement. "Is this the lady you were telling me about?"

Brad nodded.

"She is pretty, just like you said."

"More than just pretty, son. Beautiful," Brad corrected, his tone virtually demanding some response from the silent woman at his side. When Melody continued to say nothing and refused to meet his gaze, he tried to press the issue. "Melody," he said pointedly, "Hans, this is my son, William Bradley Wainwright."

"It's Billy, Daddy," the boy interrupted impatiently.

"Excuse me. Billy, then."

With Melody staring at her hands in stunned disbelief, Hans tried to cover the awkward moment by solemnly shaking Billy's hand. The youngster giggled with delight as he grasped the huge hand held out to him. Within moments the two were well on their way to becoming fast friends, as Hans promised to teach Billy to ski after the first snow in the fall.

With his son happily chattering, Brad leaned closer to Melody.

"What's wrong?" he asked, genuinely puzzled.

"Wrong?" Melody gasped, unable to keep the betrayal she felt from her voice. "What could possibly be wrong?"

As Brad's startled expression threatened to turn into a quick burst of anger, she managed to bring her voice under control. "I'm sorry. I just didn't know. You never said anything about being married or about having a son."

"It never came up."

"Where's his mother?"

"On a plane heading back to London, as far as I know," Brad said with an amazing lack of interest.

Suddenly the pieces of the puzzle fell into place.

"Lesley?" she whispered, her voice almost choking on the question.

Brad's face was a tightly drawn mask, as he nodded.

"Oh, my God. You and Lesley," she gasped, her voice ending in a small cry, as though pleading for him to deny the truth of it.

At last, as though finally grasping something of

her torment, he nodded, but he was unable to meet her eyes.

Melody stood up shakily, her eyes blurred with unshed tears.

"You'll have to excuse me," she murmured brokenly to the startled Hans.

As she stumbled away from the table and practically ran from the room, the two men stared after her, one of them confused and alarmed, the other dismayed at the distress his words had wrought.

Seven

Melody thought of nothing except her own shattered illusions, as she bolted from the dining room. She was oblivious to the commotion she was causing. She wanted only to be alone, far from this man whose love was suddenly so far out of reach.

In her room she pulled a pillow from her bed, then curled up on the sofa, clutching it in her arms for comfort. Dry-eyed now, she stared blankly into space, trying to absorb the meaning of what Brad had told her. Certainly the words had been clear enough. He was a married man and a father to boot. How could she have been so blind, so stupid? Or was it just that she hadn't wanted to see?

Surely all the evidence had been right there in front of her, in Lesley's possessiveness, in the way she had laid claim to Brad from the moment of her arrival. That sort of certainty came only with an on-going relationship, one in which both parties were bound, if not by the legality and implied permanence of marriage, then, at the very least, by the bonds of a strong emotional commitment.

She tried to convince herself that it didn't matter, but it did. It hurt deep down inside her, in a part of her heart that had never before been touched by another human being. It was as though she had lost something very precious.

How could she go on working with Brad, she wondered. She doubted if she could mask the pain she was feeling, and that pain would be increased tenfold if he were able to sense it and were, as a result, to pity her. In fact, that would be the most unbearable part of all, to see pity in his eyes, when on a few occasions at least she had been so certain she had seen longing in his look.

Hours later, it seemed, still lost in thought, she didn't hear the tapping on her door, when it began. As it became more insistent, she glanced at the clock and realized that indeed her trancelike state had gone on until the middle of the night.

"Melody, I know you're in there. Answer the door." Brad's voice was muffled, but she could hear its edge of anger.

"Go away."

"I'm not going anywhere until we talk, so if you don't want me to wake up the entire inn by breaking down this door, you'll open it at once."

Knowing he would do exactly that, she flung open the door, then walked back to her place on the sofa, refusing to look at him.

"I trust this macho mood of yours will pass," she snapped. "I don't think I'm quite up to it."

Closing the door gently behind him, Brad stood and regarded her silently for several minutes before crossing to tower over her, his hands on his hips.

"I think you owe me an apology, Miss Adamson."

"I owe you an apology," she sputtered indignantly. "How dare you?"

"How dare I what?" he asked, his voice so cool that for a moment it stilled the rising heat of anger in Melody. Looking at him for the first time, she realized with some amazement that he truly was furious. The full measure of his wrath silenced her next retort.

"That's better," he noted with satisfaction, as she calmed down. "Now, the apology."

"For what?" she asked sullenly.

"You and I made a bargain, when I agreed to give you this assignment, Miss Adamson. There were to be no emotional outbursts, no jealous rages."

"Is that what you think tonight was all about? A jealous rage?" she asked, trying to sound convincing in her indignation.

"Wasn't it?"

"Hardly," she retorted with what she hoped would come across as a truthful tone of denial. "I have no reason to be jealous of you. Your life is your own."

"That's right. It is. And if you can't manage to keep that in mind, you'll be on the next flight back to Berlin. Is that clear?"

"Perfectly clear," Melody replied at last, her voice barely above a whisper.

"I'll let that do as an apology, then," Brad said, nodding with satisfaction, as he sat down beside her.

Every fiber of Melody's being was aware of his presence only inches away, even though she fought to maintain a facade of indifference. Her hands nearly trembled with the desire to reach out and caress the lithe, muscular leg that stretched out beside her. Clasping her hands tightly together in her lap, she tried frantically to resist the urge to give in to her impulses.

There was a speculative gleam in Brad's eyes, as he watched her studied avoidance of him.

"Melody," he said huskily, his voice provocatively low. "Come closer."

Forcing her to comply, his arm circled her shoulders, pulling her into his embrace. Then, he was kissing her with the greedy passion of someone long denied.

"My God, you are so beautiful," he whispered, when at last his lips freed hers. "I want you. You know that, don't you? You know that I want to make you mine in the only way a man can possess a woman?"

Brad's words, combined with the assault his hands were making on her body, teasing and kneading her flesh into a fiery awareness of her own desires, suddenly shocked Melody into action. She leapt from the sofa as though from the reach of a dangerous flame.

"Stay away from me," she screamed. "How dare you come in here and try to make love to me only a few hours after telling me that you are a married man and not only that but the father of a son as well? How could you?''

Whether it was her words or the edge of desperation and despair in her voice that reached him, Brad looked instantly contrite.

''All right. I think I owe you an explanation,'' he said finally.

''You're damn right you do, but I doubt there's anything you can say that will change the facts.''

''Perhaps not, but at least I can give you all of the facts. Will you listen?'' The last was said in a tone of such humility and appeal that it quieted Melody's outrage. Although she hated the idea of hearing any more about Brad's marriage to Lesley, it was impossible for her to ignore the entreaty in his voice.

''I'll listen,'' she replied softly.

''Thank you,'' he said simply. He left the sofa to walk to the window and stood silently for a long while, his back to her. When he began at last, his voice was quiet and empty of emotion.

''Lesley and I met about ten years ago. She was a reporter for a small television station in the Midwest, and I was passing through town to promote a collection of my articles that had just been published. She interviewed me for the local news. The interview extended through dinner and on through the night,'' he said flatly, offering no excuses for his actions.

''It probably would have ended right there, but she came to New York a few weeks later and called. We went out a few times, and she mentioned she'd been trying to get an interview at one of the networks for a job. I arranged the interview."

"Was she just using you to get the job?" Melody asked, wincing at the flash of pain her question caused Brad.

"It's possible," he admitted, "but at the time she didn't seem the type. It never occurred to me she was anything other than what she seemed . . . a young kid with a lot of dreams."

Melody suddenly didn't want to hear another word about this beautiful young girl, who had obviously brought so much heartache into Brad's life. Mutely she shook her head, as though to ward off any more of the memories Brad was ready to share with her. But unaware of her silent appeal, he continued.

"Lesley got a job at the network. Not a very good one at first, but it didn't take her long to find a way to impress her bosses. Her rise to the top was very rapid," he said bitterly.

"Are you suggesting . . ." Melody began, unable to complete the outrageous thought Brad's words had implied.

"No," he said, immediately grasping her meaning. "Not that. At least as far as I know. She advanced on her journalistic merits, her uncanny ability to find that one splashy, sensational news story that would assure her of air space every night. That's the way you get ahead in television news, contrary to the myth that you can sleep you way to the top. You might get one job that way, but you won't keep it unless you can produce."

Brad had returned to the sofa by now and sat

slumped over, his face buried in his hands. For several minutes a heavy silence hung over the room. When Melody was able to bear it no longer, she forced herself to ask, "What about you? Where did you fit in?"

"At first I was her entrée into the so-called media celebrity circles. Globe-trotting magazine writer and beautiful television reporter, a dashing couple. The gossipmongers in New York were practically drooling over the romance. If we'd gone to every gallery opening and every restaurant at which we'd supposedly been spotted, neither of us could have done a lick of work."

"I thought you hated that sort of thing," Melody said, recalling her impression of a man who clutched his privacy about him like a warm, woolen cloak.

"I did. And I probably wouldn't have put up with it for a minute, except that Lesley was basking in it. She couldn't wait to get the papers every day to see if we'd made the columns.

"By then we were living together, and her excitement was something I was unwilling to destroy. It all seemed harmless enough anyway. I guess I found her need for attention a little amusing. I had no idea that it was some sort of desperate appeal for the love that had been lacking in her childhood."

Melody found it difficult to reconcile the glamorous, successful Lesley she had so recently met with the image of a deprived, love-starved child. Her curiosity aroused, she asked, "What was her childhood like?"

Brad's expression grew thoughtful.

"You know, to this day I know very little about it. It's something she won't discuss. Her mother died when she was very young. Her father was some sort of blue-collar worker, construction maybe. From the few things she ever said about him I gather he enjoyed his role as widower to the hilt and that there was little time for a daughter."

"He didn't abuse her, did he?"

"Not in the way you mean, but I think his attitude must have been a form of psychological abuse. The man just plain neglected her, and there was no one around to step in and fill the gap."

"She must have been a very lonely child," Melody said, for the first time feeling some measure of sympathy for Lesley as she thought of her own wonderful Aunt Leah. For a few minutes she allowed her thoughts to drift back to her own childhood, trying to imagine what it would have been like had her aunt not been there for her. How lost and alone she would have been!

With a sigh of thankfulness, Melody returned to the present. Watching Brad, who was still lost in memories of his own, she wondered aloud, "What on earth made you decide to get married, if there were already so many signs of trouble in your relationship?"

"Lesley found out she was pregnant," he told her, his eyes so filled with pain that Melody wanted to weep for him. His voice was hushed and strained with the tension of those long-buried agonies as he added, "She wanted to have an abortion."

He slammed his fist into the cushion of the

sofa, leaving a deep impression in the velvet fabric.

"God, how I hated her when she told me that. I was so angry I think I could have killed her. We fought about it for days. I was terrified to let her out of my sight for fear she would go through with it."

Even now his features were contorted with anger as he recalled those bitter, violent arguments. Melody could share some small sense of his outrage, but surprisingly she found herself understanding something of what Lesley must have been going through as well.

Hesitantly she spoke up. "But don't you see, Brad, she must have been terrified to bring a child into the world. If her own childhood was so horrible, she must have dreaded the thought that it could happen to her own child. She obviously wanted a career very badly and she was envisioning being forced to give that up. The alternative would be to neglect her own son or daughter as she had been."

Brad nodded wearily. "I understand that now, but at the time all I could think about was that she wanted to kill someone who was a part of both of us. I wanted that child. I wanted the chance to be a father. Oh, I would have chosen the timing and the situation more carefully if I could have, but I was prepared to accept things the way they were and make a life for the three of us."

"How did you get her to change her mind?"

A wry smile tugged at Brad's lips. "I simply wore her down, I guess."

Melody gave him an understanding grin. She knew how impossible it would be to thwart him, once he'd set his mind to something. Certainly she would never want to try. He had the power to sway her with the slightest glance of entreaty. A full-scale onslaught such as the one he must have launched against Lesley would crumble her resolve even more quickly.

As Brad continued, reliving the memories of the hasty wedding, the gossip-column speculations, and Lesley's growing depression about her career, Melody allowed the words to wash over her. She could absorb no more. Her mind had seized upon the painful new knowledge that Brad, this stong, willful man she had come to love in so short a time, was already married. Her mind toyed with the knowledge, tossed it about this way and that just as a puppy plays with a new bone.

What in God's name was she to do? How could she end these feelings that, despite their newness, were already so deeply ingrained in her heart that they seemed always to have been a part of her?

A sudden click flashed deep in her mind, and she recalled the numerous times Aunt Leah had hinted of an early romance that had nearly destroyed her life, a love for a married man that had tormented her for years. By the time Melody had come to live with her, the affair was over, but the bitterness and anguish lived on.

Aunt Leah's warnings had been explicit: Stay away from married men. No matter how strong the emotional pull, the physical attraction, it was never worth it. Never, she had repeated emphatically.

That warning reverberated in Melody's head, excluding all other thoughts. Finally, as though coming back from a great distance, she began to hear Brad's rambling, disjointed words once more.

"When Lesley was offered the London bureau job, we had another monumental row. This time, though, she won. She convinced me that Billy was so small, it really didn't matter where we lived, that it would be foolish to give up such an incredible opportunity. I finally admitted that I could work out of London as easily as New York. Two weeks later we were across the Atlantic, living in an idyllic little cottage about an hour by train from Piccadilly Circus."

Melody could picture just such a cozy place from her own months in London. It would have had a fireplace, leaded windows that sparkled on sunny days, and a collection of furniture supposedly discarded from someone's attic. In the States that cast-off furniture would make an antique-lover's mouth water. Outside the cottage garden would be a gay profusion of wild flowers, growing with weedlike abandon. There'd even be a small vegetable patch.

Still envisioning her imaginary country cottage, she said, "It sounds wonderful."

Brad looked surprised by her words.

"Wonderful?" he asked bemusedly. Then, with a slight shrug, "I suppose it was at times, though Lesley spent less and less time with us there. She was constantly off on one assignment or another. Billy hardly knew her. The house-keeper was more like a mother to him."

"And that became a source of irritation for you?" Melody asked perceptively.

"Yes. It did." Brad's response was defensive. "Billy deserved a full-time mother."

"And you deserved a full-time wife?"

"Yes. That too. We managed to last out a year, with the arguments growing increasingly bitter. Finally, thankfully, we both had enough sense to realize it was futile to maintain a charade of a marriage that had been a mistake from the start. One night Lesley announced very quietly that she'd given me the son I wanted and she consid-ered her duty done. She walked out the door and filed for divorce the next day, granting me full custody of Billy."

Melody could barely hide the spark of hope ig-nited by those last words. 'You mean that you and Lesley . . . I thought from the way she talked that . . ."

"That we were still married? No. Not for several years now. It's just that every now and then she decides that maybe she made a mistake and she waltzes back into my life."

At last Melody was beginning to understand the anger and resentment she had witnessed in Brad when Lesley had turned up unexpectedly in Ettal. And, if Brad, with all his insight and wis-dom about Lesley's problems, could not under-stand or accept her erratic behavior, how could Billy even begin to comprehend it? For the first time she felt desperately sorry for that tough, feisty little boy she'd met earlier in the evening.

"Was Lesley with you in Munich, when you met Billy's plane?" she asked.

"No. She refused to go to the gate. In fact, I think the only reason she decided to get back to London at all was because she knew Billy was coming today. She can't bear to see him. It tears her apart with guilt."

"But what about Billy's feelings?" Melody asked, furious on the child's behalf. "How can she do that to him?"

Brad shook his head. "I think, or I hope anyway, that Billy has somehow wiped all that pain from his memory. He was barely two when she walked out, and he hasn't seen her since. Once in a long while he'll ask about mommy, about why she had to go away. I've told him about her job and I've tried to convince him that she still loves him very much, but I'm not sure he accepts that. At least he's asking about her less and less now."

Melody was unsure how to phrase her next question or whether she should even ask it, but it was something she had to know.

"Are you still in love with Lesley?" she asked finally.

Brad looked at her a long time before answering, as though sensing that his response meant a great deal to her, perhaps too much, in fact.

"No," he said firmly, simply.

Melody's heart began to race at the look in his eyes as he spoke to her, adding, "But she is the mother of my son, and for that reason alone she will always be important to me."

There was a warning implied in those words

that extinguished the flame of hope burning in Melody. In its place now, there was an icy chill of despair.

Eight

In the predawn hours following Brad's departure from her room, Melody had tried to sort out everything she had learned in the past twenty-four hours. Never before had she been taken on such an emotional roller-coaster ride, plunging deep into despair, climbing slowly back toward a pinnacle of happiness and joy, only to be plunged back down into a gloomy pit of depression.

She clung desperately to the look she had seen in Brad's eyes, a look that seemed to speak volumes about caring and desire, even as she heard him warning her away. Like a child, fascinated with a flame even after being told it can burn, she felt herself drawn inexorably toward him. She would face all of the dangers willingly, take all of the consequences, if only she could be held safely in Brad's arms once more.

Realistically, though, she knew she faced a

long wait for an uncertain ending. Brad clearly had not let go of his past, and with Billy there as a constant reminder, it was doubtful he ever would. But she could try. She had to.

With new resolve bolstering her spirits, she even managed to hum a cheerful, if slightly off-key tune, as she showered in icy water that made her skin tingle. Grabbing the towel she'd left warming over a heat vent, she rubbed herself dry with vigorous strokes that left her skin a rosy pink.

Deliberately choosing a silky print blouse that plunged provocatively low, she tucked it into a pair of sleek navy blue slacks and added a wide belt that emphasized her tiny waist and the subtle flaring of her hips. A dab of perfume behind each ear, and she felt ready to take on the world again.

"Brad," she decided, "you don't have a chance."

She winked impishly at her reflection in the mirror before picking up her purse and bounding down the stairs. In the lobby, Billy at his side, Brad watched her descent with some amusement.

"You seem to be in awfully good spirits this morning," he noted, his eyes traveling from her flushed face to the skin bared by her blouse. There was an appreciative gleam in his eyes at the hint of firm, rounded breasts beneath the soft material.

"Can we eat now, Daddy? I'm hungry," Billy announced with a scornful look at the adults, whose minds were so obviously on other things.

"What?" Brad asked, as though a little dazed. "Oh, breakfast. Of course, son. We were just waiting for Melody. Now that she's here, we can go on in."

"I'm sorry I kept you waiting," Melody apologized to Billy, who ignored her smile and marched off, his tiny back ramrod straight.

Brad shrugged at the child's sudden burst of temper. "I think he must have gotten up on the wrong side of the bed," he said. "Don't let it get to you."

"Of course not. I'm sure he'll be fine, once he gets something to eat. Hungry men are often not accountable for their actions."

"You can say that again," Brad mumbled softly, his eyes moving over her in a way that said his own hunger had nothing to do with food.

As they joined Billy at the table, Melody tried to find a way to reawaken the spark of interest she had first sensed in him when they had met the previous evening. But he pointedly ignored her attempts at conversation throughout the meal and spoke only to his father or sat in sulky silence.

Frustrated with her inability to reach the boy, Melody grew increasingly uncomfortable. It was obvious, too, that Brad was growing irritated with Billy's behavior and that an explosion between father and son was not far off. Deciding that she had to head that off at all costs, she tried a new approach, hoping to discover the source of the child's anger.

"Billy, did I say something to offend you?" she asked directly, almost relenting when she saw the guilty look in those dark eyes, which he must have inherited from his mother. For a moment he only stared at her in confused silence, then he turned to his father.

Seeing no reprieve from that quarter, he mumbled at last, "No."

"Then what is it? Maybe, if we talk about it, you'll feel better."

For a few seemingly interminable seconds it appeared that obstinacy would win out. Melody was about to retreat into silence herself, when Billy finally spoke.

His soft, little voice a hesitant cry that seemed on the verge of tears, he asked, "Was my Daddy with you all night?"

"What?" Melody and Brad asked in startled unison.

Looking at his father, his resentment no longer masked, Billy said, "I woke up last night and looked and looked for you, but you'd gone away. Were you with her?"

"Yes," Brad said honestly. "I was with Melody for a while. We had some things to talk about. I had no idea you woke up. Why didn't you tell me this morning?"

"Because . . . because I didn't want you to get mad at me for getting out of bed."

"Why on earth would I do that?"

"Jenny does sometimes."

"Well, I'm not mad about it. I'm just sorry I wasn't there. You weren't scared, were you?"

"No," he said haughtily. "I'm not a baby."

"Of course you're not," Melody inserted quickly. "But it's always a little frightening to wake up in a strange place. I still feel funny sometimes, when I wake up and it's all dark and I can't tell for a minute where I am. I can remember when I first went to live with my Aunt Leah, I'd wake up and be afraid that she'd gone away and left me. Deep down, I knew she would never do that, but, for just a minute, I'd be a little scared.''

Clearly surprised by this admission from a grown-up, Billy repeated with interest, ''You'd be scared?''

''Sure. Everybody's scared sometimes. It's impossible to go through life feeling safe and secure every minute. And there's nothing wrong with admitting it, either. Only very foolish people try to pretend they're never afraid.''

''I guess I was afraid that Daddy had gone off and left me last night,'' Billy confessed. ''Just for a minute, though.''

Brad's words were reassuring. ''Billy, you know I'd never do that. Even when I have to go away on an assignment, Jenny always knows exactly where I am, so you can find me, if you need me.''

''I know,'' Billy said with a small sigh, indicating that his awareness of the truth of his father's words didn't necessarily translate into total acceptance of them.

''Then what's the problem?'' Brad asked, checking the impatience in his voice at Melody's warning shake of her head.

''Mommy left and never came back,'' Billy said flatly, tears welling up in his eyes and threatening to overflow.

The two adults exchanged a look of understanding, as Brad searched for words that would allay Billy's fears.

"Son, not everyone in the world is going to treat you the way your mother did. Certain things were important to her, but that doesn't mean she didn't love you. Nor does it mean that I will leave you, as she did. You are the most important person in the world to me, and I will always be there for you. You must believe that. It's a promise."

When Billy continued to look disbelieving, Brad asked insistently, "Have I ever broken a promise to you?"

"I guess not," he responded slowly.

"Okay, then. And I never will. Now let's get out of here and get started on our drive. We don't want to waste a beautiful day worrying about something that will never happen."

Taking Brad's lead, Melody quickly suggested that they go on to the car, while she ran up to her room for her cameras. When she met them in the parking lot a few minutes later, she asked Billy, "Have you thought about what you'd like to do today?"

"I want to have a picnic," he said enthusiastically. "Where I can feed the ducks."

"Then a picnic it shall be," Brad agreed. "Though I can't promise you there will be ducks."

As they drove slowly toward Munich, where Billy would catch a flight home to London at the end of the day, they wound through gently sloping countryside. They passed through several tiny villages, still slumbering on this early Sunday morning.

Melody, studying the guidebook Brad had loaned her, announced, "We're not too far from Benediktbeuern. There's an ancient monastery there that might be interesting."

"What's a monastery?" Billy asked from the backseat.

"It's a big church," Melody simplified.

"More than that," Brad interrupted. "It's also a home for the priests. They live there and study. Depending on their order, they may do special kinds of work. Some of them even make wine and sell it to support the church."

"Can we stop? I want to see it," Billy pleaded.

"Sure. We're in no hurry," Brad readily agreed. "This particular monastery might be worth a mention in the article anyway. I haven't had a chance to get here before. I'll look around and talk to some people, and Melody can take some pictures."

As they drove into the town, they had no trouble locating the monastery. A large crowd, much larger, it seemed, than the town's recorded population, was headed in that direction. Parking the car, they joined the throng walking toward the abbey church.

Suddenly they realized that the steady surge forward had halted just outside the church gates. People were packed along the sidewalks, as though waiting for a parade. Sure enough, moments later a group of young girls in heavily embroidered Bavarian costumes paraded past, followed by men in lederhosen, vests, and feather-trimmed caps. Priests in lavishly designed vestments came next, as carved religious statues and crosses were held high.

When the last of the marchers had passed through the gates to the churchyard, the crowd fell into step behind them. Melody, thoroughly entranced by the spectacle and solemnity of the occasion, was trying to capture something of its atmosphere on film. Billy was clapping and dancing about in his excitement. And Brad was watching them both with tolerant amusement.

As the choir sang, horns blared and guns rang out in a moment of colorful local pageantry that drew the three of them into its embrace. Melody's eyes were sparkling with delight by the time the service, unlike any she had ever seen before, had ended.

"Wasn't it wonderful?" she exclaimed. "Serendipities are the most fun of all on a trip."

"What's a ser . . . serpedip . . ." Billy asked, his tongue twisted on the long and unfamiliar word.

"A serendipity is finding something unexpectedly, something you weren't looking for at all."

"Like finding a penny on the street?"

"Something like that," she agreed, as Brad captured her hand in his.

Lightly he asked, "What about falling in love?"

Momentarily at a loss for words, confused by his question and the impact of his touch, Melody finally managed a whisper. "That's the best serendipity of all."

Brad squeezed her hand before releasing it and

returning his attention to Billy, who was trying to pull him in the direction of the buglers.

Left alone to puzzle out the importance of Brad's casual question, Melody quickly grew irritated with herself. She was seizing on even the most flimsy evidence to convince herself that a relationship with Brad might be possible. She had to stop that. Illusions would accomplish nothing. She had to face the truth of their relationship and its future, whatever it might turn out to be.

Finally she forced her thoughts back toward her work, shooting pictures of the small clusters of people still gathered in the churchyard. Her effort at concentrating paid off, and by the time Brad and Billy came to look for her, she had her thoughts, if not her emotions, under control again.

Back in the car, their morning's unexpected diversion behind them, they told jokes—Brad's so horrible that Melody thought her sides would split from laughter.

"I thought you were supposed to be some sort of reasonably sophisticated gentleman," she said, giggling. "Where did you ever hear such rotten puns?"

"Rotten," Brad said indignantly, his eyebrows lifting. "Billy, do you hear that? the lady says my puns are rotten. What do you think?"

"I think they're silly," Billy announced, traitorously siding with Melody.

"Silly? My own son," Brad said, shaking his head in mock dismay. "In that case I will just have to abandon my unappreciative audience right here. You can find your own ride to Munich."

With that announcement, he pulled to the side of the road.

"All right. Out with you both. I can't possibly keep two such ungrateful people with me a moment longer."

"Oh, please, no," Melody begged urgently between giggles. "Sir, you wouldn't leave us out here, would you? We might starve to death. Or be shot by hunters."

"Or be eaten by wolves," chimed in Billy.

"Surely you wouldn't inflict such a fate upon us," Melody said, giving him her most appealing smile.

"Well," Brad said with a heavy sigh of submission. "I suppose I might relent just this once. But," he added sternly, "I expect unqualified, absolutely hysterical laughter at every one of my jokes from here on out."

"We promise," Billy and Melody swore simultaneously.

The lighthearted banter continued as they stopped to pick up sandwiches for their picnic along the banks of a wide, blue lake. As they ate, they watched as several young boys tried to learn to waterski.

"Daddy, I want to do that," Billy begged.

"Nope, son. You're not quite old enough. Besides, the water is icy."

"Please, Daddy," Billy said beguilingly. "You could take me."

Melody could sense Brad's weakening resolve.

In addition, she had seen the glimmer of excitement in his eyes, as he'd watched the boys. He was dying to get up on those skis himself.

"Okay," he said, relenting. "I'll see if they'd mind letting us join them."

After a brief consultation with the teenagers, he waved for Billy to join them. Melody followed.

"You're going," she said, not really surprised at his nod of assent.

"Of course. Want to come along?"

"No, thanks. I think I'll just observe from right here."

As Brad began to unbuckle the belt on his jeans, Melody looked momentarily horrified. Catching her expression, Brad grinned wickedly.

"Don't panic, Miss Adamson. I've got a bathing suit on under here."

"Do you always dress that way, just in case you happen upon an inviting lake?" she inquired curiously.

"No. Sometimes I don't wear anything," he teased, chuckling at her furious blush. "Actually, my sweet, innocent one, I had a feeling Billy was going to want to swim today, so I came prepared. You'll notice that he's dressed for the occasion, as well."

Sure enough, Melody turned to find Billy beside her in his bathing suit, holding out his clothes for her to keep. She took them, then retreated to a shady spot on the bank, as father and son went to join the German youngsters.

Seated on a soft mat of pine needles, she watched as Brad showed Billy how to get up on the skis, applauding when he finally mastered the skill and took a brief ride totally on his own. But, as they continued splashing about in the water, she was overcome with exhaustion. Rolling Brad's jeans into a pillow, she lay back and promptly fell asleep.

When she awoke much later, judging from the shadows cast by the sinking sun, she found Brad stretched out on a towel at her side watching her.

"Sleeping Beauty's awake at last," he murmured, before leaning slowly toward her to meet her lips in a lazy kiss. His fingers trailed through the curls of her hair, coming to rest just under her chin. With his thumb, he traced a tingling path across her lips. The heat from that slight touch warmed Melody's chilled body, spreading a fiery glow along her limbs.

As Brad pulled her more tightly into his embrace, making contact along the full length of her, she moaned softly with pleasure. Arching naturally toward the hardness of his well-muscled body, she found her hands moving lightly along the silky, taut flesh of his waist, coming to rest on his back.

With a slight movement, Brad shifted her onto her back again, his lips leaving the sweetness of her mouth to edge downward along the bare skin exposed by her blouse. Pushing the silky material away, his hand slipped inside to cup her breast, which reacted instantly to his touch. When Melody gasped and tried to move away from the source of these pleasurable, though frightening, sensations, he stilled her retreat by pinning her with the full weight of his body.

"Brad, no," she pleaded, a note of panic in her voice. "Please, no."

For a moment she thought he hadn't heard, but when she tried again to squirm from his grasp, she was able to slip away. She knew he had allowed her to go, for it would have been impossible for her to escape his erotic trap had he not been willing. Not only was he too strong, but he knew just how to manipulate her into submission.

There was a look of mocking amusement on Brad's face, as he watched her inch away from his reach, struggling to compose herself and rearrange her clothing.

"Where's Billy?" she asked, hoping to divert his attention.

"Asleep in the back of the car," he reassured her. "We won't be interrupted."

"I wasn't worried about interruptions," Melody insisted.

"Oh?" Brad asked with feigned innocence. "What then?"

"I wasn't worried about anything," she said curtly. "I'm just not in the habit of making love out in the open . . . like a couple of animals, who have no self-control."

"Where are you in the habit of making love?" Brad said, seizing on her comment with undisguised glee.

"I didn't mean that I . . . Oh, forget it," she snapped, as he laughed aloud at her confusion. "You know, Bradley Wainwright, you're too damned sure of yourself."

Suddenly sobering, after all of his teasing, he

shook his head. "No, my sweet—where you're concerned, I'm not sure of myself at all."

With that admission, he leapt to his feet and pulled on his jeans and shirt. Melody sensed a sudden shift in his mood and studied him curiously, but he refused to meet her gaze. Instead, he said, "Come on. Let's get out of here before we make Billy miss his flight."

Billy, worn out from the fresh air and the afternoon's activity, barely roused up when Brad started the car. Without his chatter from the backseat, the drive into Munich was strangely silent. On several occasions, Melody wanted to break the mounting tension in the air, but the scowl on Brad's face prevented her from speaking out.

Melody was more disturbed than she was willing to admit even to herself by the sudden shift in Brad's mood. The change from lighthearted companion to a brooding, silent one was confusing and somehow threatening. It all seemed tied, too, to her refusal to give in to his physical demands. She knew that he was more than casually interested in an affair with her. Her reluctance no doubt puzzled him.

At the same time, she knew he would never allow his own feelings to go any deeper and, knowing that, it would be sheer folly for her to give in. That would surely doom forever any possibility of a more fulfilling, long-term relationship.

And yet, she told herself miserably, perhaps it was all she could hope for. Wouldn't a short-term affair with a man she loved so desperately be better than nothing?

"No," she said adamantly, not realizing she had spoken aloud until Brad turned to her, curiosity written on his face.

"Sorry," she mumbled. "I was just thinking out loud."

"Sounded to me as though you made an important decision about something. Want to talk about it?"

"I don't think so," she said uncertainly, trying to gauge what his reaction would be if she were to be perfectly honest with him and explain all of her doubts.

"Suit yourself," he said with a shrug, turning his attention back to the highway, which was leading them into Munich. Weaving his way carefully through the evening traffic, he finally found a parking place in an area filled with restaurants and beer halls.

At Melody's questioning look, he explained, "I thought we'd grab something to eat before Billy's flight. I think you'll both enjoy the beer hall. It's raucous, but early in the evening there's still a family-style atmosphere and the food's good."

Inside, the noise level was nearly intolerable, as a roving band of musicians performed, joined by the enthusiastic patrons, whose appetite for singing was clearly as lusty as that for food and drink. When Brad agreed that they would be willing to share a table with others, they were led to a second-floor room, where they were seated with half a dozen Germans celebrating a birthday.

Happily including them in their family group, the young couple and their four towheaded youngsters offered Brad, Billy, and Melody some of their cake. Soon they were all joining in the singing and the boisterous toasts, with Brad translating when Billy and Melody couldn't follow the conversation.

Melody was taking pictures through it all, delighted to see Brad's short-tempered mood was giving way to the charming, outgoing mood she loved. But, as the evening wore on and the time for Billy's departure grew near, she saw once again that hint of despondency that had been surfacing throughout the day in the form of curt, abrasive comments. There was a look in his eyes, especially when he held Billy in his lap, that tore at Melody with its mixture of tenderness and pain. She tried again and again to catch the look on film, but she had no idea if the camera could capture such subtleties of expression.

"Well, pal, I think it's about time to get you to the airport," he announced reluctantly to Billy.

"Do we have to go?" Billy asked, his voice plaintive.

"I'm afraid so." Turning to Melody, he added, "Did you get all the pictures you wanted?"

"Yes. I just want to get an address for the Reichmanns, so I can send them copies."

Brad translated her message, and the couple beamed with pleasure, as they wrote it down for her.

"You come visit," they said in halting English, gesturing to all three of them. "Any time. We make you welcome."

"Thank you," Melody said sincerely, chuckling as Billy shyly shook hands with all of the children, except the rosy-cheeked baby, who was gurgling happily on his mother's lap.

Talking about his new friends kept Billy's mind off his impending departure during most of the trip to the airport.

"They said maybe they'll come to see me someday in London, didn't they, Daddy?"

"Yes. They did say they'd try."

"Do you think they will?" he persisted.

"Maybe, son. Melody has their address, so you can always have Jenny help you write a letter inviting them. Even if they can't come, you can keep in touch."

Billy's excitement began to wane as soon as they parked the car and started toward the terminal. Carried now in Brad's arms, he was clinging tightly to his father's neck.

"Daddy, I don't want to go back. Can't I stay here with you and Melody? I won't be any trouble. I promise."

"Son, we've already talked about that. You know it's impossible. But I won't be away much longer. Before you know it I'll be back in London, and we can go any place you like."

"Will Melody come back with you?"

There was a silent appeal in Brad's eyes, as though he was begging her to find the right words to make Billy's departure easier. More than anything, Melody wanted to comply, but she didn't honestly know what to say that would help. She had no idea if she would ever see this child again, and the thought of him disappearing from her life was almost unbearable.

Finally she managed a reply. "Billy, I promise that the next time I come to London, I will come to see you and that we'll go somewhere really special."

"When?" Billy persisted.

Now it was Melody's turn to appeal to Brad. Catching her look of entreaty, he said, "Melody's very busy, son. She has to go on assignments, just like I do. But I'm sure she'll be in London one of these days, and when she comes, she'll keep her promise to visit."

At the gate Brad went with the reluctant Billy onto the plane. Watching them go, Melody felt her eyes filling with tears. He was such a sweet, lonely boy, she thought, wishing she could take him in her arms and mother him until all of his fears were chased away. His need appealed to her maternal instinct, but, more than that, he was a part of Brad and she couldn't help being irresistibly drawn to him because of that.

At the sight of Brad coming toward her again, his expression grim, she hastily wiped away the traces of tears and tried to smile. There was barely a pause in his long strides as he reached her and headed straight for the airport exit.

His only words were a tersely uttered, "Let's get out of here," as he passed.

Angry at his brusqueness, Melody trailed along behind, trying to rationalize this latest mood. She knew he was upset about sending Billy away, that he felt guilty about it, but it still bothered her that he was apparently going to take it out on her.

Biting back the heated retort she wanted to

make, she said only, "Will the housekeeper be there to meet Billy's plane?"

"Of course," he snapped in a tone of reproof that immediately silenced any further questions.

Brad's stony facade continued on the long drive back to Ettal, as he focused his entire concentration on the highway, which was blanketed in the total darkness of a moonless night. Unwilling to risk another sharp retort, Melody tried to nap, hoping that when she woke again Brad's good humor would have been restored.

Initially, though, she found sleep to be elusive, as her thoughts tumbled chaotically in search of an answer to the dilemma Brad's attitude had created for her. When at last she did drift into a restless sleep, her concerns translated into an alarming nightmare in which Brad and Billy were joined by Lesley, and the three of them walked out of her life, slamming an impenetrable, vaultlike door in her face. The look on Lesley's face as that heavy door shut solidly behind them was triumphantly mocking.

Suddenly Melody was aware that she was being shaken awake.

"Melody, come on, honey. Wake up. It's okay," Brad said soothingly, his expression alarmed. As Melody looked around in confusion, he added, "You sounded as though you were having a nightmare."

Shaking her head, as though in that way she could clear it of the memory of that mocking look on Lesley's face, she whispered in a small, slightly frightened voice, "That's exactly what it was. A nightmare."

"Would it help to talk about it?" Brad asked solicitously.

She shook her head. "No." Then, changing the subject, she asked, "Where are we?"

"We're almost back at the inn. Are you sure you're okay?"

"Fine. Really," she assured him, immediately regretting her quick response, as he started the car again and retreated behind the wall of silence that had been between them for hours.

For several miles she tried to work up the courage to break through that wall, but she finally gave up all thought of any sort of conversation as the inn loomed ahead of them.

"What's the use," she thought with a sigh of regret, as Brad turned into the driveway.

In the lobby a few minutes later, he wished her a curt good night, with barely a glance, and marched off toward the dining room, leaving her to stare after him in consternation.

"All right, Bradley Wainwright, I don't have to take this from you," she muttered at his retreating form. "You can damn well roast in hell before I will spend another sleepless night worrying about you."

Nine

The next morning Melody woke to sunlight streaming in the windows and the scent of lilacs in the air. Throwing open the door to her tiny balcony, she stepped outside and took a deep breath of the cool morning freshness. She felt surprisingly relaxed after the previous day's tension, and, as she gazed out at the distant mountains, a feeling of well-being crept over her. Perhaps her oath to put Bradley Wainwright and the conflicts he aroused out of her mind was working.

Then, from the terrace down below, she heard his voice, stiff with politeness.

"Brinkerhof, what are you doing here?" he was asking. Melody couldn't see his face as he spoke, but she could hear the haughtiness and anger in his voice. It was a tone that had not been used in his earlier encounters with Hans, and it surprised and dismayed her.

"Herr Wainwright, you asked me to join you today," Hans said quietly. "Don't you recall? Since today will be your last day in Ettal, you suggested I spend it with Melody. I am grateful for your thoughtfulness."

"I'm afraid that won't be possible, after all. We have a lot of work to finish up today and we can't afford any distractions," he said in a tone of dismissal.

Listening from her balcony, Melody was horrified at Brad's high-handedness, particularly in light of Lesley's prior interference in their planned work schedule. Hans could hardly be any more trouble than she had been. On top of that, Brad was the one who had invited him to come along today in the first place. This sudden reversal was the height of rudeness.

Rushing indoors, Melody yanked on the first pair of jeans and sweater she came to. Splashing cold water on her face and brushing her teeth quickly, she then ran a comb through her tangled curls. Not bothering with makeup, she tore out of the room and down the stairs, hoping to intercept Hans before he acquiesced to Brad's wishes and left.

As it turned out, though, she needn't have worried about Hans giving up so easily. As she neared the door to the terrace, she could hear the men arguing, with Hans trying to pacify Brad into a more rational frame of mind.

"Herr Wainwright, please, I will not be any bother, and it is important for me to see Melody once more before she leaves Ettal. We have things to discuss, plans to make."

"What sort of plans?" Brad asked suspiciously.

"For the future." The response so startled Melody that she almost gasped, but then Brad was speaking again, and she stood riveted to the spot.

"You and Miss Adamson have no future, Brinkerhof," Brad said, his voice tight with anger. "You might just as well run along back to your ski lodge and leave her alone."

"Herr Wainwright, I think it is for Melody and I to decide what our future will be, not you. So, if you don't mind, I will just sit here and wait for her."

With that declaration made, he planted himself firmly in the chair opposite Brad. The older man was so shocked by Hans's refusal to leave that, for once, he seemed uncertain about what to do next. Melody might have laughed at his confusion, had she not been so outraged by his behavior.

The two men were still scowling at each other when she began her hesitant approach. Unsure how she planned to handle the situation, she knew only that Brad's attitude was inexcusable and that it could not go unchallenged. Taking a deep breath for courage, she stepped out onto the terrace and gave Hans a beaming smile. As he leapt to his feet, his eyes lighting with pleasure, she knew what she had to do.

"Hans, darling, I'm so glad you're here already," she said enthusiastically, pausing to give him a kiss on the cheek before sitting down next to him.

Barely nodding in Brad's direction, she put a well-manicured hand on Hans's arm and leaned over to whisper in his ear how much she was looking forward to their day together. Inwardly she chuckled at Brad's barely disguised attempt to hear her soft-spoken words.

"I was just telling Herr Brinkerhof that it will be impossible for him to go with us today," Brad inserted sharply.

"Oh, no," Melody said with obvious regret. "Why?"

"We have too much to do," Brad said curtly.

"I'm sure Hans understands that we have work to finish. You won't mind that, will you, Hans?"

"No. Of course not. It will give me a great deal of pleasure just to be with you."

"Miss Adamson," Brad began, his tone like ice, "you may recall that our bargain requires that you put all of your admirers on hold for the duration of this assignment. Now will you please explain all of that to Brinkerhof, so we can be on our way."

"Brad, be reasonable," she asked quietly, managing to stem the tide of rage that was boiling up inside her. Even through her anger, she sensed that he was not prepared to be reasonable at all, and his next remark confirmed that.

"You heard me," he said insistently, standing to tower over them. "I will expect to see you at the car in half an hour—alone. That should be sufficient time for you to say your good-byes."

With that he abruptly turned and strode away, leaving them to watch him with puzzled expressions.

"Your Herr Wainwright, he seems to be in a

rare temper this morning," Hans declared in a masterful piece of understatement. "What is bothering him?"

"I don't know exactly. He's been like that since yesterday," Melody responded slowly. "I can't imagine what's gotten into him. I think it has something to do with sending his son back to London alone last night. He feels that he is constantly abandoning Billy."

"I suspect it is something else entirely, my little one."

"What?" Melody was curious.

"If I had to guess, I would say it has something to do with you, not his son," Hans said, taking her hand in his.

"With me? No, I'm sure it has to do with Billy."

"Perhaps he is worried about his son," Hans agreed. "But it is you who is on his mind today. He acts very much like a man who is jealous. He does not want me around, because he wants you to himself."

"Nonsense. Brad is not the least bit interested in me," Melody denied quickly. Too quickly, perhaps, for the perceptive Hans.

"Do you care for him so much, then, little one?" he asked softly, studying her face closely as she sought to phrase her response carefully.

"No," she insisted. "He is an arrogant, difficult, stubborn male chauvinist. I could never care for someone like that."

"I am glad to hear that," Hans said, his eyes warm as they gazed into hers. "Then, perhaps there is hope for me after all."

Melody could barely stand the look of pure yearning she saw on Hans's face. How could she bear to hurt this kind young man, who had been so attentive and friendly over the last few days?

"Hans, you are a wonderful man, and the woman you love will be incredibly lucky," she began sincerely.

"Then you are the lucky one, Melody, because I have come to love you very much. I know we have known each other only a few days, but I sense in you a kindred spirit, someone with whom I could share the rest of my life."

"No, Hans. Please. I'm not the right woman for you. I am fond of you. I will always remember our time together here and I hope that we will always remain friends. But," she emphasized, "that is all it can ever be."

Hans was reluctant to accept that. "Give it time, little one," he pleaded. "Let me show you what our life here could be like."

"It won't work, Hans. Believe me, it just won't. I wish to heaven it could," Melody said with a heartfelt sigh, her voice choking at the end as she turned to hide her tears.

For a moment, Hans's manner was frosty. "It is Herr Wainwright who separates us, who makes it impossible for you to love me, is it not?"

When Melody didn't answer, his tone softened. "I am sorry, my little one. I guess I should have known it from the beginning."

Melody's eyes lifted to meet his, her lashes damp with tears. "You won't say anything, will you?" she begged softly.

"Not a word," he promised. "He is a very fortunate man. I hope he realizes that."

Melody shook her head, her expression still sad. "I don't think there is any hope for it, Hans."

Forcing her to face him, he said insistently, "Listen to me, little one. If this morning's behavior is any indication at all, it is only a matter of time. Herr Wainwright may not be ready to admit his love for you quite yet, even to himself, but it will come. Be patient and don't give up hope."

Melody managed a weak smile at Hans's words of encouragement, but she didn't dare to take them too seriously. Besides, she admitted aloud, "Patience has never been one of my strong points."

Hans shrugged. "He is worth waiting for, no?"

"Of course."

"Then you will wait," he said matter-of-factly, adding softly, "as I would wait for you, if I thought there were any hope at all."

'Oh, Hans," Melody began, her voice a gentle cry of protest.

"Ssh. It is okay. I meant only that my love for you will not die so quickly. If you ever need me, I will be here for you, as your friend, if that is what you wish."

"You truly are a remarkable man, Hans," Melody said sincerely, kissing him softly. Reluctant to leave the security of the warm relationship she had come to share with Hans, Melody stayed by him in companionable silence, until at last she knew it could not go on.

"I suppose I can't put it off any longer. Brad will

be in a positive rage if we don't get to work. I really don't think you'd better come along," she said regretfully.

"I agree. It would only infuriate him more," he said, adding with a devilish grin, "Of course, that might be just what he needs."

Melody's laugh rang out, as she took Hans's hand and walked with him into the lobby. As they stood by the front door, she looked up at him fondly.

"Good-bye, my friend," she whispered softly, reaching up to give him a light kiss.

"Be happy, little one," Hans said, drawing her into a tight embrace. For a moment his lips on hers sought out a more impassioned response, but, finding none, he released her slowly. Without a backward glance, he turned and walked away.

Lost in the tenderness and sadness of that moment, Melody did not see that Brad had come down the stairs into the lobby in time to witness Hans's farewell embrace. He stood watching from the shadows, his face contorted with pain and anger.

Ten

Still lost in thought as she stared after Hans, Melody did not hear Brad's approach. Suddenly his gruff voice penetrated her reverie.

"Get your bags packed," he ordered abruptly.

Startled, she was sure she had misunderstood him.

"My bags," she repeated, a look of confusion on her face.

"Are you having difficulty understanding English, now that you're spending so much time with your young German?" Brad asked sarcastically. "I don't know that I can say it any more plainly: I want you to pack your bags."

"Why?" Melody's confusion was now complete.

"I should think that would be obvious," he said impatiently. "We're leaving."

"But I don't understand. I thought we had

more work to do here," she said, a feeling of desperation engulfing her. She felt her fragile hold on Brad's attention slipping away. If he sent her away now, would they ever be together again, she wondered.

"Are we just moving on to another city?" she asked, clinging to a tenuous last straw.

Brad quickly shredded that flimsy hope. "You are going back to Berlin," he responded curtly.

"But I don't understand," Melody began again.

"My God, woman, can't you just do as you're told," he snapped, losing all hold on his patience. "Pack your bags and be at the car in half an hour."

With that he stalked away, eliminating any chance of appeal. Numbly, Melody stood looking after him for several minutes, refusing to believe what she had just heard. "How can he do this," she wondered. Only moments before he had been insistent that they get started on their day's work.

Unable to find an answer to that, she slowly climbed the steps to her room, her anger mounting with each step. Slamming the door behind her, she jammed its bolt into place, then leaned heavily against it, tears streaming down her face.

Pounding her fist against the heavy, ancient wood in frustration, she murmured, "Damn him! Who does he think he is, ordering me around like some servant who gets paid to do his bidding?"

An ironic twist of a smile touched the corners of her mouth for a fleeting second.

"Of course," she admitted unwillingly, "that's exactly what I am to him: a servant. Only I take his pictures, instead of cooking his meals or darning his socks. 'Snap this, Melody. Shoot over here, Melody. Can you get that building just so, Melody?' Hell, he might as well be telling me to dust under the beds.''

Working herself into a rage, she began gathering up her clothes and camera equipment, stuffing them mindlessly into their cases, not caring what sort of jumbled mess she created. She could sort it all out later. She only prayed she could sort out her emotions as easily.

The trip to Munich was made in strained silence, no better than the drive to Ettal had been the night before. Neither of them was willing to voice feelings, for fear the anger lurking just below the surface would overcome them completely, if it were ever unleashed.

Melody clung to the thought that this rift, whatever its cause, could be healed with time. Surely something that had occurred so unexpectedly could disappear just as quickly. She ignored the nagging inner voice that commanded her to pinpoint the cause. Without that information, it said, there could be no hope for a resolution.

At the airport Brad bought her ticket and handed it to her.

"You'll be leaving in twenty minutes. Your gate is down that way," he said unemotionally, making no move to accompany her.

"You're not coming to Berlin?" Melody forced herself to ask, even though the answer appeared clear.

"No."

She ignored his tone to ask, "Where will you be going?"

"Back to London," he said curtly. "You'd better get going or you'll miss your flight."

Desperate for a clearer understanding of what was happening, she ignored his advice and persisted. "London? To see Billy?"

"That's part of it," he said, turning abruptly and starting to walk off.

She called out to him, and the panic in her voice halted him momentarily. "Brad, what about the rest of the article?"

"I'll call you," he promised vaguely, refusing even to turn and face her.

As he strode out of sight, there was nothing for Melody to do but accept it and go on to her own gate. Running as she heard the final boarding call, she was breathless by the time she arrived, and, once on the plane, she sank gratefully into her seat.

She accepted a glass of wine with the lunch placed before her, hoping it would calm her nerves, but the food remained untempting and untouched. The gnawing emptiness in the pit of her stomach could not be filled with chunks of beef, noodles, and pastry.

Back in Berlin, she took a cab to her apartment, hoping to find solace in its familiarity. But, to her surprise and dismay, she found little comfort in the chintz-covered chairs and gleaming, dark-wood antiques she had chosen with such care. Not even her favorite photographs, framed and hung along the corridor between the living room and bedroom, were able to cheer her, as the endless days of waiting dragged on.

And so, she buried herself in her makeshift darkroom. For hour upon hour, day after day, she stayed in the kitchen, its window covered over with a specially designed blackout board, and processed her film from the trip to Bavaria. She took professional pleasure in the quality of her work. All of the shots were good; some were spectacular, and there were enough of the latter, she felt certain, to assure her future once the magazine appeared.

But in the long hours at night, the satisfaction and pride she felt at having done her job well dimmed, and she tossed and turned restlessly. More often than not, she padded about the apartment in the middle of the night, her mind examining over and over every word she had exchanged with Brad, every glance. It was as though she searched for a missing clue that could unlock the puzzle of just when it had all gone so very wrong. But there was nothing there to tell her. Nothing.

She was out marketing early one morning, after another sleepless night, when she ran into one of her neighbors.

"Melody, where have you been?" Alexi cried out in her enthusiastic manner, as she rushed to embrace her friend, kissing her on each cheek in the European tradition she had adopted immediately upon getting off the plane from Georgia two years earlier.

A secretary at the American embassy, Alexi was a bubbly, outgoing twenty-two-year-old, whose intrinsic innocence and perpetual surprise at life's twists and turns constantly amazed Melody, as they did everyone else who got to know her.

This unusual side to her nature was seldom revealed, however, for Alexi preferred to maintain an impenetrable facade of frosty sophistication, which seemed more suited to her slim, stylish beauty.

"It weeds out the fainthearted men," she had admitted with a giggle, when Melody had questioned her about the incongruity during a night of sharing girlish confidences.

Now, though, her delight at Melody's return was evident. "I'm so glad you're back. Come home with me now and have some coffee. You can tell me everything that's happened. Was it exciting?"

Unable to resist Alexi's exuberance, Melody felt her spirits lifting just a bit, as she dropped off her packages in her own apartment and climbed the single flight of stairs to Alexi's. Although the layout of the two apartments was exactly the same, there was no comparison in the tastes of the inhabitants. While Melody's was slightly faded, warm, and comfortable, Alexi had filled hers with the modern glass and chrome furniture and colorful, splashy artwork that matched her public personality.

By the time Melody arrived, the smell of perking coffee filled the air, and huge chunks of apple strudel were on plates on the kitchen table. Melody shook her head at their size.

"I swear I don't know how you do it," she said

with a laugh. "You eat like some sort of dock worker and still manage to look like a model for *Vogue*."

Alexi grinned. "It's the long legs," she said. "They're empty, and it takes an awful lot just to fill them up."

"Well, one of these days you will, and you'll be sorry about all those times you gave in to your cravings for strudel, whipped cream, and big slabs of buttered, home-baked bread."

"Never. I will grow fat and sloppy, and my husband will love me anyway," she said with such certainty that the two of them burst into laughter at the image of this lovely creature someday looking plump and dowdy.

For the next hour, Alexi kept Melody amused with her tales of the personal intrigues at the embassy. It seemed two of the secretaries were dating the same diplomatic officer and discovered it by accident during an exchange of confidences one day over lunch.

"You should have seen the looks on their faces," Alexi said with a giggle, as she recalled the scene. "Later, though, they said Randy's expression was even funnier, when he arrived to pick Gloria up for their date and found Nancy sitting in the living room sipping a glass of wine. He hasn't been near either of their offices since and he goes bright red with embarrassment if anyone mentions either of their names."

"Sounds to me as though he got exactly what he deserved," Melody said, with a light laugh.

"Exactly," Alexi agreed. "Now, then, what about you? What was this mysterious assign-

135

ment you rushed off to take? Your note wasn't very specific.''

For an instant Melody's face clouded over, but she recovered quickly. Briefly, she filled Alexi in on the details of the magazine assignment, trying to avoid any mention of Brad or the personal attachment she felt for him. But Alexi, for all of her innocence, was very perceptive. Melody had learned early in their friendship that there was little she could hide from her.

''Who's the man?'' she asked now.

''What man?'' Melody replied with feigned nonchalance, hoping to steer her off the track. She should have known better than to even try.

''I'm not sure. But there is one in the picture somewhere. I can tell. And you're trying very hard not to talk about him.''

''Well, I was working with a writer, Bradley Wainwright,'' she admitted reluctantly. ''But that's all there was to it.''

Clearly unconvinced, Alexi said only, ''I see.'' Melody wasn't at all sure she did, but she was thankful that Alexi intended to drop the subject at least for the moment.

In fact, she moved on to discuss a party planned for that evening. ''Why don't you come with me,'' she suggested. ''You might make some contacts for your business,'' she added, knowing that argument more than any other might win Melody over.

Despite that urging, Melody said, ''I don't think so.''

''Come on. You can't expect to get any new assignments if you stay locked up in that darkroom of yours. Besides, the party will be fun, and you look as though you could use some."

Reluctantly, Melody gave in. It seemed easier than arguing, especially in the face of Alexi's logic and persistence.

"Terrific. I'll stop by your apartment about eight."

That night Melody took extra care with her appearance, hoping that Alexi's antidote for the gloomy mood she'd been in would work.

A full dirndl skirt she had bought in a little shop in Oberammergau made her slim figure seem almost fragile, and the off-the-shoulder blouse with its ruffle added to the femininity of the look. She brushed her hair until it curled in wisps around her face and sparkled with golden highlights. Applying her makeup sparingly, but to good effect, she managed to overcome her pallor and achieve the appearance of a healthy glow. But none of the care could erase the sadness from her eyes.

Apparently, though, that mysterious, lost look, combined with her petite, frail appearance only made the men at the party want to rescue her and protect her from whatever demons had made her unhappy. One by one they tried to charm her, and one after another they failed, having to content themselves with no more than an occasional glimmer of a smile.

Watching this distressed Alexi even more than her earlier conversation with Melody. When yet another of the young men had walked away from Melody's side, she joined her.

"Hey, pal, what have you got that I haven't? Every man in this room has tried to win you over tonight."

"I think it's their knight-in-shining-armor fantasies. They seem to think I need rescuing," she said with a slight chuckle.

"Don't you?" Alexi asked, her tone light but her look penetrating.

Melody felt her friend's concern. "Perhaps," she admitted at last. "I think I ought to go home, though, before I put a damper on everyone else's evening."

"No, please, Melody. Stay a little longer."

"Not tonight, Alexi. I'm not up to any more," she insisted wearily.

"Then I will come with you," Alexi said decisively.

"That's silly. There's no reason for you to spoil your evening just because I've got a case of the blues. Stay here and have a good time."

"Nope. I'm coming with you. It's no use arguing. Besides, I see most of these guys every day, and there's not a one of them I'd take on a bet. They're nice enough, but there aren't any sparks, if you know what I mean."

"I know exactly what you mean, but if that's the case, why did you come?" Melody asked curiously.

Alexi shrugged. "You never know when a brushfire may suddenly flare up."

Together, then, they slipped away from the party, after thanking their hostess. On the way home, relaxed now that they had escaped the party's forced gaiety, they stopped for a glass of wine.

Once they were settled into a booth, their dry white wine on the table, Alexi began determinedly. "Okay. Let's have it. What is really going on with you? I can't stand seeing you so unhappy."

Slowly at first and then with a torrent of words and tears, Melody poured out the whole story of her trip with Brad, of the growing attraction she felt for him, of his casual passes and then his abrupt dismissal of her from his life.

"Perhaps your friend Hans is right about him," Alexi suggested reflectively. "Possibly he found himself more involved than he meant to be and needed some space, some time to think things through."

"I would like to believe that," Melody said with a wistful little sigh, "but I don't think it's very realistic. No, I think the only thing for me to do is pick up where I was before I ever met him and get on with my life, as though he doesn't even exist."

"Of course you must get on with your life, but don't abandon hope quite so easily, my friend," Alexi cautioned, her words an echo of Hans's advice. "If this man is all you say he is, then his love is not something to toss aside so quickly."

"I'm not tossing his love aside," Melody said angrily. "That's the point. He doesn't love me. He may want me now and then, but that's it. Should I waste my life praying it will grow into something more?"

"Your life? No. But a few more weeks wouldn't hurt," Alexi said wisely.

Those words resounded in a cruel, mocking refrain in Melody's mind the next week, when she picked up a London newspaper at a downtown stand. On one of the society pages she found, as she glanced through it in a restaurant, there was a picture of Brad and Lesley together at some British media event. Brad was smiling down into Lesley's upturned face, his arm draped possessively around her shoulders. Dark and devastatingly handsome in his tuxedo, he was the perfect foil for the slinky designer gown in a glimmering silver material that she wore.

The boldfaced caption below the picture read: "Famed magazine writer Bradley Wainwright and international television correspondent Lesley MacDonald (the former Mrs. Wainwright) appear well on their way to a reconciliation. Word around town is that the globe-trotting couple will retie the knot any day now."

Upon reading that final bit of gossip, Melody was attacked by a sudden wave of nausea, and she fled to the rest room at the back of the restaurant. She felt better after throwing up, but her appetite was gone and her complexion pale as she returned to her table and immediately asked for her check. The waiter, his face filled with concern at her tear-dampened appearance, rushed to comply.

"You are okay, Fräulein?" he asked solicitously, as he walked with her to the door.

"I'll be just fine," Melody assured him.

"Let me get you a taxi, just the same," he insisted, hurrying to the street to hail one for her. Helping her into the backseat, he shut the door gently and leaned in the open window. "Do not worry yourself, Fräulein. Your young man will make things right."

Melody felt an outbreak of hysterical laughter coming on, as she realized what the waiter meant. He thought she was pregnant! It was the only explanation he could imagine for the sudden illness and the crying. Thank God, though, that he was wrong. Things were far too complicated and heartbreaking as they were.

At home she tossed aside her purse and tote bag, the offending newspaper crumpled and jammed into it, and collapsed onto the sofa. Exhausted by the strain of the last few weeks and the devastating news she'd just read, she fell into a deep sleep, as though her body was deterined to help her escape the pain she felt when awake.

Hours later she was awakened by the sound of someone pounding on the door. Momentarily confused, it took several minutes for her eyes to adjust to the darkness in the room. She couldn't seem to recall whether it was the middle of the night or simply early evening.

"Melody, are you okay?" Alexi called out loudly, her voice frantic. It was the note of panic that brought Melody to her feet at last.

Opening the door, she said sleepily, "What's the matter with you? I'm just fine."

Alexi's gaze traveled over her rumpled clothes, tousled hair, and tear-streaked face.

"In that case, remind me never to stop by on one of your bad days. I'm not sure I could take the shock of your appearance."

"Thank you very much," Melody said with a weak attempt at a grin. "I was taking a nap."

"You look more as though you'd been fighting a war . . . and lost."

"Thanks again."

"Don't go taking offense. I didn't mean anything. It's just that Mrs. Lendl saw you coming in earlier and said you looked pretty hysterical. She was worried about you, but didn't feel she should intrude. When you didn't answer your door just now, it scared me."

"I'm sorry," Melody said, sincerely apologetic. "But, really, I am okay. At least, now I am."

"What was the problem earlier, then?"

Melody pointed to the tote bag. "Take a look," she suggested, heading for the kitchen. "I'm going to make some coffee. Want some?"

"Sure."

Alexi opened up the London paper and instantly spotted the picture of Brad and Lesley. Carrying it with her, she followed Melody into the kitchen. "I see the problem."

"Despite what I said the other night about being realistic, I guess I wasn't quite prepared to see the truth in black and white," Melody admitted, sitting at the table and sipping her coffee.

"I've been worried you'd find out," Alexi said at last.

"What do you mean?" Melody asked, her voice registering her shock. "Did you know about this?"

Her look was accusing, as she awaited Alexi's reply.

"Well, not the part about the reconciliation exactly, but I had seen a couple of items in the gossip columns since you told me about Brad."

"Why didn't you tell me?"

"I didn't want you to get upset over nothing. You know how these gossip things are, one tenth fact and nine tenths innuendo. There could have been nothing to it, and you'd have been hurt for no reason."

"It appears that there's something very definite to it."

"Not necessarily," Alexi insisted.

"Oh, stop trying to pacify me, Alexi. I've got to face the fact that it's over. Whatever hope I had of Brad loving me is useless now. Lesley's won. And, who knows, maybe it's for the best. At least Billy will have a whole family again. He deserves that."

"From what you've told me about Lesley, I doubt they'll achieve the sort of family atmosphere and harmony you're envisioning. I don't believe in miracle cures for what she's got . . . a healthy case of selfishness."

Deep down Melody agreed with Alexi's assessment, but there was nothing to be gained by harboring any false illusions or expectations. Even if this second marriage between Brad and Lesley worked no better than the first one, it would do her no good to wait around for another divorce. As she had told Alexi earlier, she had to get on with her life, if only she knew how to do that.

Perhaps she should go back to New York. After all, she had traveled a lot these last months, learned to live on her own, and, most important, she had proved she could succeed as a photographer. She had nothing more to prove—to herself or her aunt. Maybe it was time to go back and settle down. A retreat to that loving environment in which she'd grown up might be just what she needed.

She glanced over to catch a worried frown on Alexi's face.

"You're not still concerned about me, are you?"

"Shouldn't I be?"

"No," Melody said with a certainty she was far from feeling. "I'll bounce back in no time. In fact, why don't we go out tonight?"

If Alexi was surprised by this suggestion and the sudden mood reversal, she managed to hide it. She accepted the idea wholeheartedly.

"Why don't I call a couple of the guys from the embassy? They're always ready to go out on the town. Besides, they've been mooning around over you ever since the other night anyway. This will be a way to put them out of their misery."

She jumped up and went to the phone, dialing before Melody could change her mind and back out.

"Great," Melody heard her say. "We'll be ready."

"It's all set," she announced, as she reappeared in the kitchen doorway. "Put on some fancy duds and be ready in an hour, okay?"

Melody nodded, trying not to let her know that her enthusiasm was already waning. "I'll be waiting."

Still, she forced herself to get ready. Putting on

a silky dress in a flattering shade of blue and a pair of high-heeled sandals, she conscientiously avoided thinking about Brad. Every time his image popped into mind, she quickly buried it, forcing herself to look ahead to the evening she and Alexi had planned. She tried to recall which of the men she'd met at the embassy party were the ones they'd be seeing tonight, but her mind was a blank.

When they arrived a short time later with Alexi, she could barely remember having met them. They were smoothly handsome and pleasant, but compared to Brad's effortless dominance of every situation, they seemed weak and very young.

Despite that, she found herself having an enjoyable time. The men went out of their way to charm her, keeping everything on a lighthearted, even keel, almost as though they had been briefed by Alexi about her need for a smooth, uncomplicated evening of fun.

They began with dinner at a neighborhood Italian restaurant, run by a family that seemed to encompass at least four generations. An old man, his weather-beaten face telling such a tale of rough living that Melody longed for her camera, dominated from his seat near the door, as his grandchildren played at his feet.

Stuffed from the mounds of pasta they had consumed, the quartet decided on a nightclub nearby, so they could walk a little. Feeling better, they watched the floor show and then danced. Melody found that she was able to keep all thoughts of Brad at bay, as she moved around and around the dance floor with her seemingly inexhaustible partners.

"Whew," Alexi muttered breathlessly, as she collapsed into her seat. "I don't think I'll ever move again."

"I'm afraid you'll have to move at least once more," the fair-haired young man named Evan Longsworth III said with a laugh.

"Why?" Alexi asked with a pained expression.

"Because this place is about to close, and I doubt you'd want to spend the night here."

"I'm not so sure. If it meant not having to move, I'd give it a try."

"Come on, Alexi," Melody encouraged. "You can make it."

Rick Watson, looking down at her appraisingly, said finally, when she made no move to get up, "Well, if you can't, you can't."

With that he picked her up as though she weighed ten pounds, instead of a hundred and ten, and tossed her unceremoniously over his shoulder.

"Put me down, you idiot," Alexi squealed, as he marched determinedly through the door and the others trailed along behind howling with laughter.

They were still caught up in the same mood of hilarity when they arrived back at Melody's apartment. While the others settled in the living room, she began scrambling eggs and making toast in the kitchen. Just as she was about to put the food on the table, the phone rang.

With all of the boisterous laughter and talk in

the living room, it was difficult for her to hear at first, and she had to repeat herself several times before she could get the caller to speak loudly enough.

"What the hell is going on there? And where have you been until this hour?" Brad demanded, his anger plain, even with the crackling that was breaking up the long-distance connection.

For an instant Melody was stunned into silence by the sound of his voice. A part of her was so relieved to hear him that she was almost ready to ignore his rudeness.

When she managed to speak at last, though, her voice was flat. "What do you want?"

"I want to know what's going on there."

"That's none of your business, Mr. Wainwright. Now, is there something I can do for you, or shall I hang up and rejoin my friends?"

"Don't you dare hang up, Miss Adamson. I want you to meet me in Rothenburg tomorrow."

"Sorry. I can't make it," she said with only the slightest hesitation.

"What the devil do you mean, you can't make it?"

"Now it appears you're the one having trouble understanding plain English," she retorted sharply. "I said," she repeated slowly, "it will be impossible for me to be in Rothenburg tomorrow. Or any other day, for that matter," she added with a surge of anger.

When Brad spoke again, his voice was so low Melody had to strain to hear him.

"I suggest you think that decision over very carefully, Miss Adamson. If you fail to fulfill our agreement on this assignment, I will see to it that you never work as a professional photographer again. The best you'll ever do is a wedding in Peoria," he warned.

"I'd rather do that than spend another moment with you," she snapped without regard for the consequences.

"So," he said slowly, "this is personal. Well, Miss Adamson, it appears I was wrong about your level of professionalism after all. I'm sorry I misjudged you. If you change your mind, you will be at the Hotel Braun in Rothenburg by five P.M. tomorrow. If you're not there, you will be replaced on the assignment."

Melody had no doubt that he would carry out his threat, but for a moment she was tempted to tell him to take his damn assignment elsewhere. She didn't need him. Finally, though, her good sense prevailed, and she said begrudgingly, "I'll be there."

It wasn't until she heard her words echoing emptily over the phone line that she realized that Brad had hung up.

Eleven

As Melody sat in stunned disbelief, the phone receiver still in her hand, Alexi came to see what was happening.

"Melody, what is it?" she asked urgently, seeing the look of dismay and pain on her friend's face. "Is it bad news?" You aunt isn't ill, is she?"

"No. It's nothing like that. It was Brad."

"Oh." Alexi's voice hovered on the edge of a question.

"He ordered me to be in Rothenburg tomorrow or lose the assignment," she said flatly, then looked up, anxiety and anguish evident in her eyes. "Alexi, what can I do? I don't think I can bear to see him knowing that he is about to marry Lesley again."

"Then don't go. It's as simple as that."

"Simple? That's hardly simple. My career depends on my completing this job. He . . . he said he'd see to it that I never worked again if I failed to live up to our agreement. And he can do it, too. I know he can."

Alexi was shocked. "I don't believe you. He wouldn't be that vindictive."

"Oh, yes, I think he would be," Melody said with conviction. "If he felt that I had crossed him, he would go to any lengths to get even. It would take only a few calls from him to the right people and my career as a photographer would be over. No magazine or wire service would ever dare to use my work again."

"Would that be so terrible, my friend?" Alexi asked softly, putting a comforting hand on Melody's shoulder.

"Terrible?" Melody repeated with a slight shudder. "It would be disastrous. Photography is the only career I've ever wanted."

"Then you have no choice. You must go."

Melody looked at her helplessly. "You're right. I have no choice," she said resignedly. Then, with gathering strength and determination, she added, "But I will never forgive him for this. Never!"

As she completed her declaration, the men joined them, curious to know why they had been abandoned. Brushing aside their questions, the two women hurried them through the late-night meal and on their way. As Alexi followed them from the apartment, she paused to give Melody a hug.

"Good luck tomorrow," she whispered. "If you need any moral support, just call."

"Thanks. I will," Melody responded gratefully.

Wide awake with nervous energy, she spent the next hour straightening the apartment, doing the dishes, and getting her camera gear together. She also packed a batch of the completed prints and color slides to give to Brad in Rothenburg. At least he wouldn't be able to argue about the quality of her work.

By the time she had run out of mind-numbing chores, it was four A.M. and she knew she had to get to sleep for a few hours at least, if she was to cope with the ordeal ahead of her with any sort of rational calm.

Up again at eight, she began the complicated task of figuring out the best way to get to the tiny, walled town of Rothenburg on the Tauber River. By taking the train part of the way and then renting a car, she just might make it in time to meet Brad's five P.M. deadline.

She spent most of the train ride engrossed in a guidebook account of Rothenburg's history. Fascinated with the story of the town, which seemed frozen in the sixteenth century with its narrow, cobbled streets, gabled houses, and the remains of two fortified castles, she read quickly. She was delighted by the story of its salvation during the Thirty Years War, when Count Tilly would have razed it, but for a taste of the local wine.

She had barely absorbed the tale of Rothenburg's colorful past when the train arrived in Würzburg, where she was to pick up a rental car for the drive to her final destination. Regretting that she had no time to visit the city's large, Baroque palace, she headed quickly on her way, her heart and stomach fluttering with nervousness as the time for her confrontation with Brad neared.

Her mind was so occupied with the thought of that ordeal that she didn't notice the gathering storm until huge drops of rain splashed against the windshield. As she drove on, the water seemed to pour from the leaden sky in solid grey sheets. Where only moments before there had been daylight, it was now dark as night and bolts of lightning flashed all around her.

Gripping the wheel tightly, she fought to keep the car on the narrow road. Although common sense told her to pull off and wait until the storm had passed, she was afraid she'd become mired in the mud and be stuck in the countryside for hours. She'd passed only one or two cars since she'd left Würzburg, so it was clear this was not a well-traveled road, on which help would be quick to appear.

Creeping ahead at a snail's pace, she tried hard to quell the rising panic that threatened to destroy her last hold on her composure. She'd never been one of those people who loved to be caught in the midst of a wild thunderstorm, delighting in the roar of nature unleashed. Now, in this tiny car, which seemed to sway dangerously with each sweep of the wind, she had never felt more insecure and alone.

The final last miles into Rothenburg seemed to take an eternity, and once she had passed through the gate to the city, she almost collapsed over the wheel with relief. Pulling into a parking place, she looked over her map and quickly got her bearings. She was only a few blocks from the

Hotel Braun, where Brad would be waiting. For the moment the thought that he now belonged to another woman was pushed aside in her desire to feel the strength of his presence.

It took her only moments to reach the hotel. Leaving the car in front, she entered the lobby, where Brad was pacing about like a caged panther, his muscles clearly outlined beneath the close-fitting material of his tan slacks. A look of relief spread across his face when he saw her, and oblivious to all of her conflicting emotions, Melody ran straight into his waiting arms.

Feeling her trembling through her cold, damp clothes, he held her tightly to him, his hands gently stroking her back in a movement designed to soothe, rather than arouse.

"Baby, are you all right? What's wrong?" he asked, his voice filled with alarm as she clung to him fiercely.

"The storm," she gasped finally. "I was so afraid. The road was flooded."

The words came out in broken gasps, as she tried to control the sobs that threatened to overcome her.

"You're okay now," he soothed gently. "I've been out of my mind ever since that rain started. I wasn't sure if you were late because of the storm or because you weren't coming at all."

"Did it matter?" she asked hesitantly, looking directly into his eyes for the first time since she had entered the safety of his embrace.

"Of course it mattered," he said gruffly. "Why the hell do you think I threatened you? I knew it was the only chance I had to make sure you'd come. Then, when you were so late, I was afraid it hadn't worked."

Suddenly he released her, as though fearful that further contact would lead to revelations he wasn't prepared to make yet.

"Come on. Let's get you to your room and out of those wet clothes. We can talk later over dinner."

Then, as a sudden thought occurred to him, he added, "Or are you too tired for dinner? Would you rather just get some sleep?"

"No, I'm not too tired. Dinner will be fine."

He guided her up the stairs then and into the loveliest room Melody had ever seen in a hotel. Filled with delicate antiques, polished to a subtle gloss, it was lit with the indirect glow of soft lamps and candles in pewter holders. The windows were draped with dusty rose velvet on either side, while fine, white, transparent curtains fluttered in the breeze that was sweet with the scent of spring flowers and air washed clean by the storm. A huge comforter encased in satin looked so inviting on the double bed that Melody wanted suddenly to slip beneath its warmth and go straight to sleep after all.

Brad did not follow her into the room, announcing, instead, that he would go to the car for her things. "You take a hot shower and by the time you're out, your dry clothes will be here."

As the hot spray of the shower soothed her tense muscles, Melody began to relax for the first time in weeks. Once more Brad had her in his power, all memory of his impending marriage wiped away by those few moments of comfort in his arms. Right now she felt she could forgive him anything, including his presumptuous demand that she make this trip in the first place.

Wrapped in an oversized towel, her hair in damp curls around her flushed face, she peeked into the bedroom. There was no sign of Brad, but her suitcase was beside the bed and dry clothes had been spread on top of the comforter. She slipped into matching bikini pants and bra in a cream-colored lace that always made her feel very feminine and slightly wicked.

Then, dismissing the idea of wearing pants and a sweater, even though their warmth appealed to her, she pulled on her clinging turquoise dress, feeling an additional boost to her spirits, as she examined her appearance in the still-steamy mirror of the bathroom.

She had just finished applying her makeup, when a knock on the door signaled Brad's return. His eyes, when she opened the door, held a very masculine vote of approval, though he said only, "I thought you could use some time to yourself."

"Thanks," she said warmly, her eyes locking with his in a timeless gaze that hinted she was thanking him for much more than his small gesture of consideration. His response was to pull her into his arms, holding her loosely as his lips sought hers in a gently insistent kiss. His tongue teased her lips into parting with a provocative touch, then invaded the sensitive sweetness within like a bee seeking out the pollen for honey.

As his embrace tightened, she could feel the

hard muscles of his thighs against hers, and a pleasant sensation of warmth began spreading through her, mounting to a feverish excitement. It was suddenly as though they were both aflame with a heat that could, at any moment, burst into an uncontrollable conflagration. That she could arouse this passionate response in Brad was a source of joy and terror to her. Her panic lay in the knowledge that this strangely contradictory man held the same power over her.

Reluctantly Brad's lips left hers. But while his arms slowly loosened their hold, they did not release her.

"As I see it, we have two choices," he said lightly. "We can leave now and go out to dinner or . . ."

"Or what?" Melody asked daringly.

"Or we can stay right here and satisfy a hunger of another sort." His voice was husky and thick with desire, as his mouth moved to the sensitive pulse on her neck.

At that instant Melody wanted nothing more than to satisfy that desire, but she knew that would be a step from which there could be no turning back. She was not ready for that. Not yet, anyway.

"I think dinner would be a whole lot safer," she said tremulously, almost hoping that Brad would argue with her. Instead, he merely nodded in agreement and led her to the door.

Hand in hand, they left the hotel and wandered through Rothenburg's twisting, cobbled streets, still damp from the earlier rain. Aimless in their search for a place to eat, they walked up and down until they came upon a small restaurant that seemed to beckon to them.

Seated inside, their glasses of wine already served and dinner on the way, they had time at last simply to talk. Oddly enough, now that they did, Melody could not find the words to ask the hundreds of questions that had been tormenting her since they parted in Munich. While she was mentally phrasing and rephrasing each one, Brad spoke.

"What made you decide to come?"

Melody suddenly wasn't sure how to answer that. She had been so sure that she had come only to save her career. Now that she was here, though, she knew she had been irresistibly drawn to see Brad again, to feel his touch and to try, once more, to thaw the chill that made those incredibly blue eyes seem like ice. But that wasn't the response she could give now.

Instead, she said, "You threatened my professional future. Or had you forgotten that little piece of blackmail?"

"No. I hadn't forgotten," he said guiltily. "But I had to be sure you would come. That seemed the only way."

"You could simply have asked," she suggested.

"I did," Brad reminded her. "You refused. Tell me the truth, though—was the threat the only thing that brought you here?"

Melody's heart was beating wildly at the predatory gleam in his eyes, but she managed what she hoped was an air of nonchalance as she asked, "What other reason could there be?"

Brad's voice dropped to a throaty whisper, as he said, "I had rather hoped that you wanted to see me as much as I wanted to see you."

Melody willed herself not to respond, but she knew from the outset that it was a hopeless idea.

"I did miss you," she said at last, her eyes lighting with pleasure as his hand reached across the table to hold hers tightly.

"Then why did you sound so angry on the phone?" he asked.

"It . . . it doesn't matter now."

"If it almost kept you from me, then I think it does matter . . . very much," he insisted.

Melody took a deep breath, as though bracing herself for an angry outburst. She would have preferred to let the whole thing drop, but Brad would never let go of the issue until he'd gotten whatever answers he needed to satisfy his curiosity.

Unable to meet his eyes, she forced herself to ask, "Are you and Lesley planning to marry again?"

The silence that greeted her question went on for an eternity, until Melody thought she would not be able to stand it for another instant. Finally, though, Brad responded slowly. "So that's it? How did you find out?"

Melody fought down a tide of hysteria at the implication that the rumors were, in fact, true.

"The papers . . ." she began, her voice trailing off.

"I should have guessed. Well, the papers were wrong. We are not remarrying," he said flatly.

Melody's silent prayer of thanks was cut short

when he added, "But, if I am to be totally honest with you, that's not all there is to it."

"What do you mean?"

"Before I answer you, let me ask you a question: What is your relationship with Hans?"

"Hans?" Melody asked blankly. "What has he to do with any of this? He is a friend. That's all. I thought you understood that."

"Perhaps that's all it was to you, but he was in love with you. I knew that. When I saw you together that last day in Ettal, I had the impression that you shared his feelings. Are you telling me that you didn't love him?"

"Never," Melody denied. "And Hans knew that. When he kissed me that morning, it was a farewell kiss, and we both understood that."

"I didn't," Brad admitted rather sheepishly. "I wanted to kill him for daring to touch you. Then, when I saw you respond, I decided you must want a future with him as much as he wanted one with you. If that was the case, the only thing left for me was to get out of your life."

Melody almost laughed at the ridiculous way in which their relationship had nearly ended.

"So that is why you sent me back to Berlin?"

Brad nodded.

"And that's why I went back to London. I thought that, if I couldn't have you, perhaps I should try once more to work things out with Lesley."

"Then you were thinking of marrying her again?"

"Yes," he admitted ruefully. "But it didn't take long for me to see that nothing had really changed for us. She is still thoroughly wrapped up in her career, and I still can't accept that. If there were only me to consider, maybe we'd have a chance, but there is Billy, and I can't allow him to suffer any more.

"Do you know that she actually left the country on an assignment without even calling him to cancel an outing they had planned? His disappointment tore me apart. I won't have it happen again."

Brad's adamant words reassured Melody that she had nothing to fear from Lesley ever again. Hope set her pulse racing, and her eyes sparkled with happiness. As they sat and sipped wine, lingering at the restaurant for hours, a feeling of contentment stole over her. Mellow now and slightly giddy from the heady mix of wine and Brad's presence, she had an uncontrollable urge to giggle, as they began to walk back to the hotel long after midnight.

"You aren't by any chance just the slightest bit drunk?" he asked with amusement, as she clung unsteadily to his arm.

"Of course not," she replied indignantly. But the sober sternness of her reply was promptly contradicted by another fit of giggling.

"Perhaps we ought to walk a while longer," Brad suggested indulgently, leading her down a narrow street lined with craft shops.

There were windows filled with leather goods, embroidered skirts and blouses, hand-blown glass, toys, and wood carvings. Melody gasped with pleasure at some of the carvings, fragile pieces so intricately worked that they appeared to have been done by one whose hands were as skilled as those of a surgeon.

"Come on," Brad insisted, when she would have lingered longer. Like a child, he tugged on her arm. "The shop coming up is my favorite."

"Why?" Melody wanted to know, reluctant to leave the treasures in front of her.

"You'll see," he said mysteriously, as he led her to the next shop and then stood back to wait for her reaction.

Melody's eyes widened with delight as they took in the hundreds of handmade Christmas decorations, from tiny, hand-carved mice dressed for the holidays to elaborate Nativity sets, from completely decorated miniature trees to huge, gaily painted glass ornaments suitable for a towering evergreen.

"It's wonderful," she cried, clapping her hands together. "Can we come back tomorrow and buy some?" she added, turning to give Brad an appealing look.

"Say please," he instructed with mock severity.

"Please," she responded softly, standing on tiptoe to seal her request with a fleeting kiss.

"When you ask like that, how could I possibly refuse," Brad said, tuckng her arm through his and holding her close to his side, as they moved on to the walled-in garden just behind their hotel. Still close together, they stood staring out into a night filled with stars, as an entire valley lay spread out below them.

Melody felt as though she had been drawn into a magical spell. It was a sensation she seemed to experience only when Brad was near, the warmth of his breath a teasing torment on the soft skin of her neck, as he leaned down to whisper in her ear.

"I'm very glad you decided to come," he said huskily, his arms slipping around her waist from behind, as he pulled her back against him.

"So am I," she said softly, not daring to turn and face him for fear the slightest movement would break the spell that had been cast over them.

Slowly his hands moved along her sides in a gentle, massaging pattern. When she made no move to stop him, they continued their erotic assault on her senses. Capturing the fullness of her breast in one hand, his thumb found the already-aroused peak at its center and began massaging it into a hardened pebble of sensitivity. It was as though an electric current was sparked by his touch, radiating a series of shock waves from that single point throughout the rest of her body. She trembled at the unfamiliar sensations.

As a tiny moan of pleasure escaped from her lips, Brad turned her to face him, his lips descending to take hers in an inevitable kiss. Pulling her tightly against him, it was his turn to tremble, as her hands began to brand him with the fire of her touch. Uncertain, wanting only to share her pleasure with him, she began a tentative but devastatingly successful assault of her own. Her hands kneaded and stroked the muscles of his back, molding his body more tightly to her own.

"Do you have any idea of what you are doing to me?" he asked breathlessly, holding her hips locked against his own. Innocent as she was, she had no doubt about what he meant as she felt the hardened muscles of his body quiver with passionate desire.

Weak with her own desire, she could only cry out softly with pleasure at the sensations that were leading her into a whirling vortex of feelings. When Brad pulled back without a word, she felt suddenly bereft until she realized that he was leading her back into the hotel.

Silently, they climbed the stairs to her room, their only contact Brad's firm grip on her hand, an innocuous enough touch that still had the ability to arouse her. Once inside, she was struck by a certain shyness, which Brad dispelled by quietly suggesting that she might want to change.

Grateful for a momentary reprieve from the physical contact that was playing havoc with her emotions, she followed his instructions. She needed some time to prepare herself for taking what she knew would be an irreversible step. With hands that trembled with a mixture of trepidation and desire, she shed her clothes, replacing them with a long, pale yellow gown. Only the barest concession to modesty, its silky transparent material actually revealed far more that it covered, hinting suggestively at the full breasts beneath the lacy pattern of the top.

Returning hesitantly to the bedroom, Melody stood framed in the light of the doorway, unaware of the picture of innocent beauty and radiant sexuality she presented. In the dim light of the room, lit now only by candles, it took her a moment to find Brad. Startled, she realized he was already in bed waiting for her.

"My God, you are gorgeous," he said throatily, the catch in his voice revealing the impact she had on his senses.

"Come over here," he commanded softly.

A tiny voice inside Melody was warning her not to comply, but she could no longer ignore the louder voice of the physical attraction and love she felt for him. She moved slowly to the edge of the bed, trying not to notice the bare expanse of his broad, well-developed chest with the burnished brown, tightly curled hairs like a mat across its center. The blanket had slipped to his waist as he turned toward her, and Melody blushed as she considered whether he was, in fact, wearing anything at all.

"You're not planning to stand there just out of my reach the whole night, are you?" he taunted her. "I don't think I could stand that."

Melody was powerless to resist his urging. He drew her down beside him and kissed her very gently, his lips moving slowly from her eyelids to each cheek, her ear, her neck, before finally claiming her lips in a long, lingering kiss. Her lips parted to his gentle probing and, as the kiss deepened and their tongues met, a violent, electrical clash seemed to explode inside Melody, and she felt herself losing all sense of time and place.

Sensing her arousal, Brad slid the yellow silk gown from her shoulders, exposing her soft, bare skin. His hands stroked and caressed until her entire body radiated with a fiery heat and trembled at each new touch.

"I want you," he whispered in a voice filled with desire. "Oh God, how I want you, Melody."

Speechless, but somehow no longer afraid of the feelings that assailed her and the step she was taking, she nodded.

"Are you sure?" he asked, his eyes looking deep into hers, as though searching her very soul for a response.

"I'm sure," she said, her voice low but firm. "I want you too, Brad."

Inflamed by her assent, his gentle but experienced hands began tracing a fiery path over her bared skin, followed in a pattern of merciless, skyrocketing torment by his lips. Melody was beyond all resistance now, giving herself entirely to the tide of passion on which she rode with him.

Her own hands, with increasing certainty, sought to create an answering response in him, moving over his chest, his muscular arms, his flat stomach and his back. She was clinging to him tightly, her desire for a culmination to their lovemaking equal to his, when he murmured, "Oh, Melody, my own sweet love, I promise you it will always be like this with us. Always."

Emboldened by his declaration, she responded ardently, "I love you, Brad. I swear to you that I will be a good wife. I would do anything to make you happy."

Suddenly Brad was still beside her, but his hands no longer making their sensual demands. Then he was up and out of the bed, pulling on his pants in stony-faced silence.

"What is it? What's wrong?" she pleaded, frightened by the look she read on his face as he stood towering over her. "Brad, please, tell me what's wrong."

"I thought you understood," he growled.

"Understood what?" she asked in confusion.

"There will be no marriage. I never mentioned marriage," he stated in a voice tight with tension and anger.

"But you said . . ." Melody began, choking on the words, "you said it would always be like this."

"Yes," he said, spitting out the words in the sharp staccato bursts of a machine gun. "Like this. No strings. No demands. I want you, Melody. There's no denying that. But I will never marry another woman who is wed to her career. Not again. Not after Lesley."

So, there it was again. Lesley. She was between them still. But now Melody's rage was equal to Brad's. Snatching up a robe to put on over her gown, she stood indignantly before him.

"Do you mean that I'm good enough for an affair, maybe even a long-term one, but that's it? That's all tonight was about?"

For a fleeting second, Brad had the grace to look embarrassed, but he spoke just as heatedly as before. "Don't make it sound like all I wanted was some cheap, tawdry, one-night stand."

"But that's exactly what you wanted, isn't it?" she demanded.

"No."

"Then what exactly would you call it?"

Brad looked at her helplessly.

"I wanted us to have a . . . a . . ."

"I thought you were the expert on words," Melody snapped sarcastically. "Are you having trouble finding the right one? I don't wonder. The only one I can think of is *affair*."

"Stop it," Brad demanded. "I wanted us to have a relationship, a lastng one. I care about you."

"No. You want me. I think you'd better leave now."

"Melody, don't do this to us."

"To us? That's a laugh. As of this moment, Bradley Wainwright, there is no us."

Digging in her bag, she came up with the pictures and slides she had brought with her to Rothenburg. "Here," she said, tossing them at him. "Take these and get out. Our 'relationship' is over."

Brad took a step toward her, his hand outstretched in a gesture of entreaty. "Melody, please."

Quickly, she backed out of his reach. "Brad, if you don't get out of here, I will," she threatened, moving toward the door.

As though afraid she might do just that, he picked up his shirt from the back of the chair, pulled it on, and gathered up the pictures from the floor, where she had tossed them. He brushed past her without another word, shutting the door softly behind him.

Melody, her eyes filling with unshed tears, didn't see the look of quiet desperation and loss on his face as he walked out of her life.

Twelve

Melody sat in the sunny dining room of Aunt Leah's East Side apartment in New York, lingering over her second cup of morning coffee, as she sorted through the Sunday edition of *The New York Times* in search of the entertainment and arts section. Her photography exhibit was scheduled to open the following Friday, and the gallery owner had told her that the *Times* had planned an advance article for the Sunday edition.

Leafing through the pages of the thick section, she finally found the art reviews, and, sure enough, there was the promised article, accompanied by a photograph from the show. It was a picture of Brad, a close-up that somehow managed to reveal everything she had ever seen in him—his rugged good looks, his strength, his humor and, deep within those dark eyes, the sadness that lurked just beneath the surface charm.

She studied it now with a certain amount of detachment, a detachment earned by the space of several months. So much had happened since she had taken the seemingly interminable trip from Rothenburg back to Berlin.

For one thing, she had decided to go home. It wasn't just that she had been gone long enough or even that she had proved herself as a photographer. She had had a desperate, crying need for the comfort only Aunt Leah could offer. She needed to be enveloped by the warmth and security of being part of a family again, albeit just a tiny family of two.

It had taken her only a few days to wrap things up in Berlin—to sublet her apartment, sell all the nonessential things she had accumulated during her three years abroad, and say her good-byes to Alexi and the handful of other friends she would miss. She had done all of that with grim-faced determination, fighting tears at every turn, holding the pain of losing Brad at bay with a will she had not known she possessed.

Aunt Leah had been delighted with her decision, when she had made the transatlantic call to let her know. But she had seen through all of Melody's logical explanations about the suddenness of it and sensed that there was something her niece wasn't saying. She was wise enough, though, to keep silent, knowing that Melody would talk about it in her own good time.

Numb with fatigue, her bruised emotions buried deep in some inner space, she had made the flight to New York oblivious to the comedy film that had everyone around her on the plane howling with laughter. She had moved through customs at Kennedy International Airport in a daze, not caring that the lines were long and only crept along or that those around her were exploding with fits of temper at the delays.

She had almost broken when she had entered the main terminal and seen Aunt Leah, her arms open wide for an embrace, her face reflecting her mix of concern and joy at Melody's homecoming.

In the taxi into the city, Melody had tried to answer her aunt's questions, all innocuous enough in their studied attempt to avoid the real issue of what was troubling the young woman at her side. But all of the attempts to keep things light and casual only made the atmosphere in the taxi more strained. They settled back, finally, into an uneasy silence, as Melody stared out at the Manhattan skyline, peaks of steel grey against a dismal backdrop of light grey haze. The gloominess seemed to match her mood.

At the apartment it had taken her only a couple of hours to unpack and settle into her old room again. After a light dinner, made awkward by her inability to make inane conversation and her refusal to discuss what was really on her mind, she had pleaded exhaustion and gone to bed, with Aunt Leah staring worriedly after her.

She had slept around the clock and she was just beginning to stir the following morning at ten A.M., when Aunt Leah had peeked in.

"You awake?" she asked softly.

"More or less," Melody replied, yawning. "Come on in."

"I brought you some breakfast," she said, placing a tray of eggs, juice, toast, and coffee in front of Melody. "Just don't get used to the service."

"Thanks."

Gratefully Melody had sipped the hot coffee, freshly perked and fragrant with a rich aroma, but the food on the tray remained untouched. When it became clear that her niece wasn't going to eat, Aunt Leah removed the tray and sat down beside her on the bed.

"Hey, kiddo, what's up?"

"Nothing," Melody said, but she was unable to meet her aunt's penetrating gaze.

"Don't give me that. You wouldn't be here, if there weren't something wrong. Not that I'm not happy to have you home. I am. I've missed you like crazy, but I know you were having the time of your life in Europe only a few weeks ago. Now, what went wrong?"

"I can't talk about it," Melody said, her voice breaking as she choked back a sob.

"I think you'd better try," Aunt Leah insisted, ignoring the pleading look Melody gave her. "Come on, baby, you always did try to hold things inside. Let it go. You'll feel better once it's out in the open."

She reached out to brush away the tears that were now streaming down Melody's cheeks. That touch, combined with the concern and love in her aunt's eyes, crumbled the wall of self-protection she had built around herself in the last couple of weeks. Sobbing, she fell into her aunt's arms and cried as she hadn't since her parents had died.

She was feeling that same sort of loss now, that

emptiness that comes when someone you love is gone, when you know that person will never be there again to talk or laugh with you, to hold you.

When all of her tears were shed at last, she had haltingly told her aunt the whole story about Brad's obsession with having a stay-at-home wife, about his insistence that the only relationship for them would have to be an affair, if she intended to pursue her career.

"I had to leave," she said brokenly. "I couldn't stay with him on those terms, knowing that there would never be any commitment, any real future."

"You did the right thing, honey," her aunt had reassured her. "You would never have been happy with him. You couldn't be content with an affair, nor would you be happy if you gave up the career that means so much to you."

"I know," Melody agreed, facing her aunt with a hurt expression. "But why does it make me ache so much inside?"

"Because it is never easy to lose someone you care about, even when you know it's for the best. Believe me, though, time will take care of that pain," Aunt Leah had promised her.

But time hadn't taken care of it. Not really. Here it was more than six months later, and it still hurt, if she were to admit the truth. Most of the time, she was able to bury the memories, but today, looking at the photograph of Brad in the paper, she was taunted by them.

There had been a few, rare times when she had been able to view this picture and others of him and Billy with a professional distance, choosing and discarding among the prints purely on the basis of her artistic instincts. But this morning the man whose eyes stared back at her from the pages of the *Times* was not simply Brad, an interesting subject, but Brad, the man she had loved and lost. All of that pain was flooding back.

As she sat lost in thought, Aunt Leah came in, poured her own cup of coffee, and cut a slice of the warm Danish coffee cake that was part of their Sunday ritual, a treat they denied themselves during the week. Noticing that Melody's slice lay untouched on her plate, she gave her a searching look.

"You okay?"

"Sure," Melody said with a forced note of gaiety that might have deceived someone less perceptive than her aunt.

'Nice try, but I'm not buying it. What's wrong?" she persisted. Then, with a flash of intuition, she asked, "Did they use that picture of Brad in the paper?"

"How did you know?" Melody was startled.

"It doesn't take a mind reader, my dear. You're sitting here moping on a glorious Sunday morning, with your very first photography exhibit getting major attention in *The New York Times*. The only thing that could possibly spoil all that would be the memory of Brad. If it still hurts so much, why did you include the picture in the show?"

"Because Daphne insisted. She thought it was the best thing I'd showed her. She was right,too."

"You still could have refused. There will be other shows."

"But it shouldn't bother me anymore now," Melody said angrily.

"There's often a huge gap between shouldn't and doesn't," Aunt Leah said gently.

Melody looked at her helplessly. "When am I going to get him out of my system?"

"When you meet somebody even more exciting and wonderful. And it's about time you did that, too."

"But I am dating," Melody responded defensively.

"Honey, who are you dating? I have never seen such an assortment of quiet, unassuming, boring men in my life. You're either determined to find the exact opposite of Brad or you're playing it safe with your emotions, knowing damn good and well that none of these men could ever interest you enough to hurt you."

"That's not fair," Melody began heatedly. "Ben and Mark especially are very nice."

"Nice, yes. And unthreatening. Sweetie, they're not for you. You can walk all over them. I doubt they feel strongly about anything, even you."

"All right. So they're not dynamic or ambitious or gorgeous. So what? They're pleasant company."

Aunt Leah threw up her hands in a gesture of surrender. "Okay. Okay. If that's all you want, then Ben and Mark and the rest will do very nicely. Just promise me one thing," she asked of

175

her niece. "That you won't marry one of them. I don't think I could bear to be around when the boredom sets in."

Melody was still indignant. "What makes you so sure I'd get bored?" she demanded.

For the first time her aunt allowed herself a trace of a smile.

"Honey, can you honestly tell me that a single one of them excites you or makes your heart race when he walks into the room? Have you ever wanted a one of them to make love to you?"

Melody looked at her aunt with surprise.

"Well, have you?"

"No," she admitted slowly. "Oh, so what? Maybe the chemistry isn't the greatest, but I've had enough chemistry to last a lifetime. God knows the sparks flew when Brad so much as looked at me, and where did that land me? Never again," she swore, starting to leave the room.

"Not so fast, young lady. Let me say one more thing, and then I'll get off the subject," Aunt Leah said, forcing Melody to return to her seat at the table.

"Chemistry may not be the most important thing in a marriage, but it is an important part. There are relationships that don't have much at the outset, but that manage to build it as love grows. Sometimes it's instantaneous. But either way, it's always there or you're headed for trouble. You may be able to fool yourself into thinking it won't matter, but be fair. Don't cheat these men too."

Although she refused to admit it aloud, Melody knew that Aunt Leah was right. She was being cautious, deliberately selecting men who posed no threat to the tentative balance she had finally achieved in her emotional life.

At first she had tried hard to feel something, especially with Ben. He was a fine man, steady, solid, dependable. And he adored her. He'd made that plain. In fact, she had a sinking feeling that he was about to ask her to marry him, and that, she knew, would spoil it all. Because, even without Aunt Leah's wise advice, she knew the answer would have to be no.

The days leading up to the Friday preview of her exhibit were filled with so much activity she was able to push all thoughts of Ben and Brad out of her mind. Although others were actually responsible for the hanging of her work, she wanted to be there to watch. She felt like a mother, who knew that her child's first babysitter was perfectly capable of adequate care but was reluctant to relinquish control nonetheless.

There were more newspaper interviews to do as well. With the *Post,* the *Daily News,* even Long Island's *Newsday.* Most of the reporters confined their questions to her training, her career up until now, her tour of Europe as a free-lancer, the magazine article she'd worked on with Brad that had been responsible for bringing her to the attention of this gallery. She was able to answer them almost by rote.

Then came the day she sat across from a sleek, sophisticated critic from a national magazine. The woman seemed to have taken an instant, inexplicable dislike to her and was making no attempt to hide it.

At first Melody thought she might be imagining the sharp edge to Arlyn Randolph's questions. They were the same ones asked by so many others, but there seemed to be a biting, sarcastic tone in her voice as she asked them. When the questioning took a sudden twist, Melody knew that she was not imagining the antagonism. This woman was heading toward forbidden territory, territory Melody refused to discuss publicly.

"What about the man in the photographs?" Miss Randolph asked. "Was he someone you knew well?"

"He was someone with whom I worked for a while," Melody responded in a voice tight with restraint.

"I know that," the woman said in a dismissing tone. "I saw the article you did together. But your photography seems to hint at a much more personal involvement."

"I don't think that's relevant," Melody said coldy, hoping to end the line of troublesome questions.

But Arlyn Randolph had not won national recognition for her writing by being intimidated by her subjects. "Were you in love with Bradley Wainwright?"

"My relationship with Mr. Wainwright is none of your concern," Melody snapped, barely controlling her anger.

"Perhaps not," the writer replied sweetly. "But I do think it adds a dimension to the article, if I can tell my readers that the photographer and her handsome model were, shall we say, close. It explains so much more about the work.''

"Well, I'm afraid your readers will have to do without that bit of added enlightenment," Melody said, rising from her chair. "I have no comment."

With that she turned and stalked from the restaurant, hoping she could escape into the relative safety of a taxi before allowing the tension of withstanding that personal interrogation to rip into her and tear apart the fragile hold she had on herself. She shook with a mixture of rage and pain as she rode the few blocks to her aunt's apartment.

"How dare she ask those questions," she mumbled aloud.

"You say something, lady?" the driver asked, his eyes lifting to the rearview mirror to glance at her.

"Just thinking out loud," she apologized.

"It's okay with me," he said, clenching his cigar more tightly between his teeth. "I get all kinds in here."

She was still seething with anger when she stormed into the apartment a few minutes later.

"What happened?" her aunt asked, looking up with surprise as the door slammed shut.

"Oh, I just got the third degree from some blasted woman who thinks her readers deserve to know all about my private life."

"I see," Aunt Leah said softly, barely smothering a smile.

"Oh, don't look at me like that. I know all that stuff about public figures being fair game for any questions. I'd just hoped I could avoid it. I thought I had too, until today."

"What did she want to know, as if I couldn't guess?"

"She wanted all the intimate details of my relationship with Brad. She seemed to feel it would add some perspective on my photography."

"She's right, too, isn't she?" her aunt chided her gently. "Those pictures reveal so much because you knew Brad so well. A stranger would never have permitted so much intimacy."

Melody sighed deeply and sank onto the sofa. "I know you're right. Maybe my hide will toughen up after a while."

"It better," her aunt warned. "This woman may have been the first to ask, but she won't be the last."

"You won't mind if I hope you're wrong, just this once, will you?"

Aunt Leah grinned. "No, indeed. Just be prepared, in case I'm right."

Fortunately, though, there were no more probing, personal interviews, and Melody dressed for the preview with a knot of nervous anticipation at the pit of her stomach. For the first time she realized exactly how far she'd come in just a few short years. Her first one-woman show in New York! Oh, how she had dreamed of this moment.

Now that it had come, though, she was feeling peculiarly flat. She was excited enough about the preview and what it said about her future potential, but there was a crucial ingredient missing: someone with whom to share it all.

"No time to start thinking about that," she muttered aloud as she put on a forest green top glittering with silver threads and gauzy, harem-style pants. It was a style she'd resisted, knowing it would soon go out of fashion, but Aunt Leah had bought the outfit for her, insisting she needed something a little daring, a trifle offbeat for her opening night.

She had just finished her makeup when the doorbell rang. When she opened the door, slightly self-conscious in her new clothes, she was instantly reassured by the smiling approval in Ben's eyes.

"You look smashing, Melody," he said appreciatively. "You too, Leah," he added, as Melody's aunt followed her into the room.

"Thanks, Ben. You look pretty smashing yourself," Aunt Leah said so politely that only Melody caught the slightly sarcastic inflection. Ben was in his usual three-piece suit in conservative grey, with a tie in muted shades of blue. He looked clean-cut, neat, and handsome, but hardly smashing. Melody gave her aunt a warning look, which the older woman ignored as she picked up her cape and sailed toward the door with an elegant flourish.

"Come on, my pets, let's get this show on the road. We can't have the star late to her own opening."

Outside the evening was crisp and clear, and they walked the few blocks to the gallery on Madison Avenue. So far the late fall nights had been cool, but without any of the dampness or icy wind that can turn Manhattan into a freezing cold wind tunnel that numbs the senses. Melody loved the buoyant feeling she got after a brisk walk on a night like this.

They arrived at the gallery with only minutes to spare before the opening. The director was almost frantic.

"Darling, you scared me to death. I thought you'd be here long before now. I was afraid you were backing out on me," Daphne said breathlessly, kissing Melody, Aunt Leah, and Ben excitedly on each cheek.

Without a pause for their explanation, she babbled on nervously.

"I just know tonight is going to be an incredible success. People have been calling all day, one gentleman in particular. I finally told him you would be here tonight, of course, and that seemed to satisfy him. Do you know any men with sexy, deep voices?" she inquired, but didn't wait for an answer.

"There's more, now. I mustn't forget anything. There are flowers for you in my office. And don't let me forget to introduce you to Maurice Hazelton. He's absolutely loaded, and, if he buys some of your work, you'll know you've made it. He has an incredible knack for picking out new talent and buying up their works early. I guess that's why he's loaded," she concluded, slowing down at last.

Just when Melody thought she would scream if Daphne said another word, the gallery's assistant manager came over to suggest they open the doors. From that moment on, Melody didn't have a moment to herself.

Although she had been to her share of openings in the past, none had really prepared her for her own. At the others she had been a guest, an interested spectator who could roam the gallery at will, chatting with others, drinking a glass of wine, and looking at the artist's work with a practiced eye.

But tonight's opening was more than a social event for her. It was a business occasion, necessitating that she meet the right people, make contacts that could help in the future and even smooth the way toward a sale or two tonight, by making the potential buyer feel important. She hated it and would have avoided it if she could, but Daphne had insisted it was imperative for a newcomer to mix and mingle.

After two hours she was ready to drop. She felt as if she had been on her feet for a week, and the excited pitch of forced gaiety was beginning to grate on her nerves, just as Daphne's chatter had earlier. She felt on the verge of a splitting headache.

Excusing herself from the couple she had just met, she slipped into the office and settled down on the plush, overstuffed sofa. Kicking off her shoes, she stretched out, hoping that a few minutes' reprieve would restore her sufficiently to get through the rest of the evening.

With her eyes closed, she massaged her temples, thinking about the chaotic scene outside. If she were to tell the absolute truth, it was not so much the pressure of meeting so many people or even the inane, nonstop conversation that was bothering her. It was feeling Brad's presence no matter where she turned. She'd no idea how powerfully she would be affected by those photographs when they were hung. They had been shot with so much love, and now, enlarged into bittersweet memories, they mocked her.

"Melody?"

At first, hearing her name whispered by that deep, resonant voice, she thought it was part of her daydream. But when it was repeated, her eyes snapped open.

"Brad?" she asked softly, as though her eyes might be deceiving her in the dim light. "What are you doing here?"

"Do you want me to leave?" he asked hesitantly.

"No," she said weakly, then more firmly. "No, please. I'm just surprised. Why did you come?"

"I couldn't stay away, not after Arlyn Randolph sent me a copy of her article."

Melody was puzzled. What could that horrible woman have written that would bring Brad halfway around the world for this opening? And why would she send it to him anyway?

"I don't understand."

"Arlyn and I used to be . . . well, we used to be involved," he said, watching her reaction.

So that was why she had been so antagonistic, Melody realized.

"But what did she write that made you come?"

"It was the pictures, as much as what she said. She ran several of them, explaining that you'd refused to discuss your relationship with the sub-

184

ject, but that any fool could see that you must have been deeply in love with him," he said quietly, as Melody uttered a small cry. "Is that true? Were you in love with me?"

Brad was still standing tensely before her, as though waiting for a verdict from a jury. He looked as though a wrong answer would send him fleeing from her life again as quickly as he had returned. Studying him before saying anything, she noted that he seemed tired and that he was thinner than he had been, though not so thin that he didn't look devastatingly gorgeous in his camel-colored slacks and designer shirt with a pin-stripe that picked up the blue tones in the camel-and-blue tweed wool of his jacket.

"Melody," he repeated. "Were you in love with me?"

"Yes," she whispered, lifting her eyes to meet his. A current of electricity leapt between them.

"And now?"

For a moment she resisted making the admission. She was still too vulnerable, and nothing would be gained by telling him that, yes, she still loved him, if he was still determined to limit her role in his life to an affair.

But, if she weren't honest, if she didn't take a chance, then all would be lost. He would walk out of here now, as surely as she had left him behind in Rothenburg. It was a gamble she had to take.

"I still love you, Brad," she said simply.

The tension seemed to drain from his body, as her words sank in, and he pulled her to her feet and into his arms.

"Melody. My love," he said, crushing her

against his chest. "I didn't think I'd ever hear those words from you. I thought I'd lost any right to ever see you, after what happened in Rothenburg. I was a fool. I know that now. Thank God for the article. It gave me hope that you might still care."

"I never stopped caring. Not for a minute," she said, feeling secure once more in his embrace, as though she had truly come home again. When he kissed her, with a hungry, demanding kiss that sent her senses reeling, she knew that she was lost forever. No matter the terms, she was his.

"We'll get married as soon as possible," he was saying now. "It can be a big wedding, a small one, whatever you want. Just so you say yes."

Suddenly he pulled back from her, his eyes fearful once more as they studied her closely. "You will marry me, won't you?"

Although Melody knew there was only one answer she could give, she asked, "What about my photography?"

"You can work as much as you like, as long as you promise to keep a very special place in your life for Billy and me and our children."

Melody's hand caressed the side of his face, as she spoke. "I promise you that you will always be the most important thing in my life. You always were. My career could never take away from my love for you. It can only enhance it."

Then he was pulling her down beside him on the sofa, his lips nibbling at her ear, tenderly touching the sensitive skin on her neck, as his hands moved in a sensuous, stroking pattern along her arms, down her sides. The heat from those strong hands seemed to burn her skin. When they moved slowly upward to claim her breasts, Melody thought she would faint with mounting desire, she arched her body towards his, gasping for breath, as every nerve ending seemed to be attuned to his expert touch.

This was the chemistry Aunt Leah had meant, and she had been right, Melody thought, as her senses careened crazily. Her heart was pounding, and beneath her own hands she could feel that Brad's was racing as well.

Then, unexpectedly, the office door was flung open and Daphne breezed in, oblivious to their guilty expressions as they broke apart.

"So," she said with mock indignation, "I turn my back for a single instant and you find yourself the handsomest man at the party. I don't suppose you're the one who called her every hour on the hour today, by any chance?"

"Guilty," Brad admitted, grinning as Melody looked increasingly uncomfortable.

Catching her expression, the gallery owner laughed. "Darling, don't be embarrassed on my account. As far as I'm concerned, you could stay in here the rest of the night and have the time of your attractive young lives. But I do think it's the tiniest bit rude to the rest of the guests. Do you suppose you could spare just a few more minutes for them, Melody, and then you can take this gorgeous creature home with you?"

"A few more minutes?" Melody asked, with a sigh of resignation. "You promise that's all?"

"Absolutely," Daphne swore, winking at Brad. "I doubt I could keep your attention much longer than that anyway."

"Okay, then, I'll be right out," Melody agreed.

Daphne nodded with satisfaction and left them alone again.

"You'd better follow your leader and get back out there to your fans," Brad said, when Melody curled her body back against his.

"Aren't you one of my fans?" she teased.

"One of your biggest fans," he agreed with a smile.

"Then don't I owe you a little special attention?" she asked hoarsely, as she pressed her lips to his. The tips of their tongues touched lightly and the rippling shock waves began again, creating a matching trembling in him.

When, after several suspended moments, she broke away from his embrace and got unsteadily to her feet, he asked dazedly, "What was that for?"

"That was my promise that this will be the last time my career ever comes first," she said, gazing lovingly into his eyes. "Now you make me a promise."

"What's that?" he asked cautiously.

"That you'll remember exactly where we left off."

ABOUT THE AUTHOR

ALEXANDRA KIRK believes romance can be a walk on the beach, a candlelight dinner for two or just a look from the right person. A journalist and former television critic based in Miami, Ms. Kirk now works at a university medical center and spends her spare time playing tennis, entertaining friends and relaxing near the water. She is the author of another Circle of Love Romance, *Sand Castles.*

CIRCLE OF LOVE

With Circle of Love Romances, you treat yourself to a romantic holiday—anytime, anywhere. Enter The Circle of Love—and travel to faraway places with romantic heroes. . . .

☐ 21502	GOLD IN HER HAIR #1	$1.75
☐ 21507	ROYAL WEDDING #2	$1.75
☐ 21508	GATES OF THE SUN #3	$1.75
☐ 21500	DESIGN FOR ENCHANTMENT #4	$1.75
☐ 21503	THE CINDERELLA SEASON #5	$1.75
☐ 21506	ASHTON'S FOLLY #6	$1.75
☐ 21509	A RING AT THE READY #7	$1.75
☐ 21504	THE RELUCTANT DAWN #8	$1.75
☐ 21510	THE HEATHER IS WINDBLOWN #9	$1.75
☐ 21538	VOICES OF LIVING #10	$1.75
☐ 21511	MIDSUMMER DREAMS #11	$1.75
☐ 21514	LOVE'S DREAMS #12	$1.75
☐ 21512	THREAD OF SCARLET #13	$1.75
☐ 21515	THE BOTTICELLI MAN #14	$1.75
☐ 21513	HERON'S KEEP #15	$1.75